COSCOM
ENTERTAINMENT

ALSO BY A.P. FUCHS

BLOOD OF MY WORLD TRILOGY

DISCOVERY OF DEATH
MEMORIES OF DEATH
LIFE OF DEATH

UNDEAD WORLD TRILOGY

BLOOD OF THE DEAD
POSSESSION OF THE DEAD
REDEMPTION OF THE DEAD

THE AXIOM-MAN™ SAGA
(LISTED IN READING ORDER)

AXIOM-MAN or
AXIOM-MAN: TENTH YEAR ANNIVERSARY
SPECIAL EDITION
EPISODE NO. 0: FIRST NIGHT OUT
DOORWAY OF DARKNESS
EPISODE NO. 1: THE DEAD LAND
CITY OF RUIN
EPISODE NO. 2: UNDERGROUND CRUSADE
OUTLAW
EPISODE NO. 3: RUMBLINGS
FROZEN STORM (SIDE ADVENTURE)
SCARLET SYNERGY (SIDE ADVENTURE)
THE SUMMONING
EPISODE NO. 4: TRANSFORMATIONS
NEW DAWN
OF MAGIC AND MEN (COMIC BOOK)

MECH APOCALYPSE

MECH APOCALYPSE

OTHER FICTION

A STRANGER DEAD
A RED DARK NIGHT
APRIL (WRITING AS PETER FOX)
MAGIC MAN (DELUXE CHAPBOOK)
THE WAY OF THE FOG (THE ARK OF LIGHT VOL. 1)
DEVIL'S PLAYGROUND (WITH KEITH GOUVEIA)
ON HELL'S WINGS (WITH KEITH GOUVEIA)
ZOMBIE FIGHT NIGHT: BATTLES OF THE DEAD
MAGIC MAN PLUS 15 TALES OF TERROR
UNDENIABLE
THE DANCE OF MERVO AND FATHER CLOWN
FLASH ATTACK: THRILLING STORIES OF TERROR, ADVENTURE, AND
INTRIGUE
GIGANTI-GATOR DEATH MACHINE: TRIPLE FEATURE
ZOMTROPOLIS: A RECORD OF LIFE IN A DEAD CITY

ANTHOLOGIES (AS EDITOR)

DEAD SCIENCE
ELEMENTS OF THE FANTASTIC
VICIOUS VERSES AND REANIMATED RHYMES: ZANY ZOMBIE
POETRY FOR THE UNDEAD HEAD
METAHUMANS VS THE UNDEAD
BIGFOOT TERROR TALES VOL. 1 (WITH ERIC S. BROWN)
BIGFOOT TERROR TALES VOL. 2 (WITH ERIC S. BROWN)
METAHUMANS VS WEREWOLVES

NON-FICTION

BOOK MARKETING FOR THE
FINANCIALLY-CHALLENGED AUTHOR
CANADIAN SCRIBBLER: COLLECTED LETTERS OF AN
UNDERGROUND WRITER
LOOK, UP ON THE SCREEN! THE BIG BOOK OF
SUPERHERO MOVIE REVIEWS
GETTING DOWN AND DIGITAL:
HOW TO SELF-PUBLISH YOUR BOOK
THE CANISTER X TRANSMISSION: YEAR ONE

THE CANISTER X TRANSMISSION: YEAR TWO
THE CANISTER X TRANSMISSION: YEAR THREE
THE CANISTER X TRANSMISSION: YEAR FOUR
THE CANISTER X TRANSMISSION: THE LONG YEAR FIVE
THE CANISTER X TRANSMISSION: THE VERY LONG YEAR SIX
THE CANISTER X TRANSMISSION: YEAR SEVEN

POETRY

THE HAND I'VE BEEN DEALT
HAUNTED MELODIES AND OTHER DARK POEMS
STILL ABOUT A GIRL
CAUGHT IN BLACK HEADLIGHTS

WWW.CANISTERX.COM

by

A.P. FUCHS

COSCOM ENTERAINMENT
WINNIPEG

ISBN 978-1-83436-006-5

Published by Coscom Entertainment

Text set in Garamond
Printed and bound in the USA

Cover art by Kevin Phillips
Cover design by A.P. Fuchs

This book is for those who have followed
THE AXIOM-MAN SAGA from the beginning.

Welcome to the end of Act One.

Thank you for flying with Axiom-man all these years.

BATTLE OF POWER TRILOGY BOOK ONE

AXIOM-MAN™

THE SUMMONING

PROLOGUE

AXIOM-MAN'S INSIDES WENT hollow at the silence. He stood atop an old nightclub in the Exchange District called The Empire. It was well past party hours. The bars and clubs had shut down around 2AM. Those who stumbled out and headed to their next destination were already loaded in cabs and in cars driven by friends who knew well enough not to mix alcohol with the steering wheel. Above, the night was clear but no stars were visible except a few poking through the dark fabric of the night; the moon hid somewhere behind a building across the way.

The quiet was a bad sign. It was almost cliché, Axiom-man thought, the idea that it's quiet—*too* quiet—meaning somebody was up to no good. That could have been the case right then; it could also mean all was genuinely well in this area of the city and all he had to do was keep watch.

The silence.

It gnawed at Axiom-man's insides, the real message shouting in his mind loud and clear: quiet means you don't know what's going on.

Not knowing made him grip the folds of his cape all the tighter as if funneling his frustration from his brain, down his arm, and into his fist clenching the light blue fabric would make things better.

His powers were of no use at the moment. Flight, energy beams, ultra strength, and even the light blue aura that subtly covered his body when his powers were activated—none of them served him in cracking the silence and learning what was really going on behind closed doors or down the deep shadows of an alley. All he had was your average sight and hearing. Nothing more.

I need more, he thought . . . then caught himself. After all this time, he knew full well his powers—*keeping* his powers—ran on responsibly using them. The messenger was behind that, that man who glowed bright blue and didn't have a face. The one who gave him his powers and changed his life.

It was a simple formula, Axiom-man discovered: use the gifts responsibly and for the wellbeing of others and they increased via a *surge* that came out of nowhere and enhanced a particular gift. But if he faltered . . . . Axiom-man hadn't done so—so far as he was aware—but knew deep down if he misused his powers, even in a way unbeknownst to him, he'd lose some—or all—that he'd gained so far.

No, he couldn't need more. Sure, more power would be helpful and he'd probably get a lot more done, but it was the desire for power he had to keep in check. He didn't know if the messenger could read his mind, but he did know the messenger could read his actions. Axiom-man would have to be careful, and not just for the sake of his powers. His own selfish need for more could be the linchpin that ended the crusade and, as a result, left countless lives in danger . . . especially with Redsaw still out there no doubt biding his time before a strike.

Murders and riots were on the rise. City officials and leaders had the brilliant solution of deploying more dangerously-armed policemen both on foot and by ride in an effort to curb the tide. Though well-intended and sensical in theory, reality dictated otherwise. Those extra men and women in uniform made a dent and controlled a few unruly events, but that was about as far as they made it before being mauled by an angry mob that overpowered them even at the cost of gunshots and chests with holes in them.

But here, up on this roof, the silence in what was supposed to be a chaotic city didn't sit well. He scanned the rooflines of all surrounding buildings, looked down and did the same for the perimeter of each he could see from his vantage point. A scant three cars had driven past since he'd been up here. The roads were vacant otherwise. Even way over in the distance, it was quiet.

With a jolt, Axiom-man spun around on the rooftop, certain someone was there to cause trouble. He lowered his fists when he saw the rooftop vacant.

Get it together. Quietly: "Paranoia never got anybody anywhere." *But what are you paranoid about?*

The answer was obvious and his mind came up with it immediately: Redsaw.

Axiom-man looked down at his boots. "But you beat him." *No, you didn't. If you truly beat him, he'd be chained up in a hole without his powers, his true face exposed for the world to see. No, you didn't beat him. You merely stalled him, and he's taking advantage of that stalling by not showing his face, though you know full well he's behind the unsolved murders, even the riots. Nothing catastrophic triggered them. Unless you count the catastrophe that is you.*

He hated it when his mind wandered and showed him a truth. He *was* the catastrophe. If it wasn't for him, Redsaw wouldn't exist. If it wasn't for that terrible night when the Doorway of Darkness opened, other events wouldn't have nearly destroyed the city.

"What's done is done," Axiom-man said, trying to regain some control of his headspace.

He approached the ledge of the building and peered down, his heart already sinking at the prospect of looking, finding nothing, the silence and inactivity getting to him once again. Instead, below, an elderly man in a scruffy beige jacket that needed a good wash and some gray slacks slowly made his way down the sidewalk. He shuffled his feet forward as if each step was a test in balance despite him holding a basic, hook-handled black cane. But, it seemed, the cane wasn't terribly relied upon given the way he set his weight upon it. More a prop than an actual tool.

Who was this guy? Why the old-man act with a cane when he clearly didn't need it?

Thanks to the riots and some brave citizens who took it upon themselves to attempt to regain control of the city, vigilantism was on the rise. There were already rumors of a figure in dark gray taking care of business.

And you're one to talk, Axiom-man thought then silently flew across the street to the building overlooking the old man. *Just make sure the guy stays safe.* Axiom-man once again scanned the surrounding area. Nothing but quiet except the old man below.

The fella didn't make a sound as he ambled down the sidewalk. No humming, no talking to himself—just a walk.

He shouldn't be out here. It's late. Either the guy has insomnia and needed to get out or he's got some kind of dementia and doesn't realize what he's doing and what the hour is. Or maybe he's got issues going on in his life that need sorting? Axiom-man didn't know and did his best not to care. He'd learned during his time wearing the cape he couldn't care for the people of Winnipeg in a genuine sense. He could care about them—even love them—as a whole but never on an individual level. To care personally about those in his city only led to heartache and cynical thinking. No, the people were the people and that was it. That was the only option to be most effective.

The old guy paused a moment, looked down for a long time, making Axiom-man wonder if the guy did indeed have something wrong upstairs and just discovered he was lost. A moment later, the man resumed his shuffle.

Footsteps, well-spaced apart. Axiom-man listened carefully. Were those the old man's or—

"Hey, old timer. Out for an early-morning stroll?" The male voice was soft but deep. He stood before the old man.

He's just a kid, Axiom-man thought. Well, not a kid. Adolescent. One with dark brown hair, a dark green T-shirt, and a set of jeans that had seen better days.

The old man didn't say anything and kept on his way. The young guy sidled up next to him and shoved his hands in his pockets. "Yeah, yeah, it can be lonely out here sometimes, huh?" The guy sounded almost casual, non-threatening.

He's luring him in, Axiom-man thought.

"Look, son," the old man said, "if it's all the same, I'd like to walk alone."

"Sure. Sure, I get it. You need some time to work things out. That's cool. I do that too. Midnight walks to clear the head. Yeah, yeah, I get it. Go right ahead. Don't let me bother you."

The old man simply nodded. Axiom-man noticed the old fellow didn't move or adjust the cane in case things went south and it needed to be used in self-defence. A subtle move that would be obvious to most.

The two kept on down the sidewalk. Axiom-man leaped to the next rooftop to keep up with them and, slowly crouching, made his way along its ledge, supervising the men below.

After about a minute, the old man stopped walking. "Sir? You're still walking beside me. I'd really like to be left alone."

At first, it looked like the young man was going to nod his acknowledgement then back off but instead leaned in close to the old man and said something Axiom-man couldn't hear.

The old man straightened.

Here it comes. Axiom-man kept his eye on the hand holding the cane. The moment the old guy swung it, he'd swoop in and put an end to a fight before it even began.

The old man faced the youth. The youth had his hand out.

"Give it," the young man said.

The elderly gentleman planted his cane and leaned upon it. Axiom-man leaned in as close as he could from his perch so he could hear what the old man had to say.

"Son, I've been alive almost four times as long as you have."

"Stop talking. Give the wallet. I walk away."

"And I've seen things that would cause your young eyes to melt."

"I said stop talking!"

"And now you're raising your voice at me. Do you not realize we live in a world where there's someone out there in a blue clownish outfit who likes to hurt people like you?"

The young guy looked around as if thinking hidden cameras were planted all around them.

Axiom-man heard the word "clownish" but knew what the guy meant. To an old dude like him, the costume *would* be clownish. Though Axiom-man referred to it as a uniform, to pretty much everyone else it was a costume, and he could only imagine that's how it was referred to in senior circles. He didn't care. The uniform served a purpose.

"That guy in blue tights isn't even around here," the youth said. "He's got bigger fish to fry. He's probably off flying around with a babe in each arm, showing them the world."

Axiom-man furrowed his brow. *Valerie.*

The old man continued walking.

"Did I say you could move?" the young man said.

The old man kept quiet.

"Hey!" The youth grabbed the guy's arm.

Axiom-man stood on the ledge, ready to jump down.

The old man paused before he spoke. "Here." He reached into his jacket and slowly produced his wallet.

The young man snatched it away, let go of the old man's arm, and tried to make a break for it. The old man snapped out his hand and grabbed the kid by the wrist. "You can have my wallet, son, but before you go, I want you to take a look at me."

The kid seemed confused.

"Go ahead. Take a good look."

The kid stared at him then glanced at the wallet.

"Congratulations. You just robbed an old man." He hefted the cane, looked at it, and Axiom-man wondered if the man's comments were a ruse and soon that cane would go flying across the youth's face. Instead, it merely remained by the old man's side.

The youth didn't say anything.

The old man didn't either. The two merely locked eyes.

"What I give to you, I give to you freely," the old man said. "But now you get to walk away and consider what just occurred." The old man let go. The young man lingered a moment then took off.

Axiom-man thought about flying down and checking to see if the old man was okay, but there didn't seem to be a need. The old man waited until the kid was out of view, took his cane, spun it around a couple times in his hands like a bo staff then tucked it away and continued his shuffle down the street.

He could've taken that kid out at any moment. But he didn't. He just handed it over, gave a short speech, and let it go.

"That man is the kind of hero I'll never be," Axiom-man said. *He planted a seed.*

CHAPTER ONE

THE MASK CAME off and Gabriel let it drop to the floor.

"What's wrong?" Valerie asked.

He looked up and took in her long, brown hair set in ringlets. The long hair thing was new, but not that Gabriel minded. Long hair, no matter the color, was always an attraction point. He had a few ideas as to why—like how the long hair accentuated the curves of the shoulders and some of the other upper curves a woman has—but also this was Valerie. The hair made her look even more beautiful and seemed to make her brown eyes shine brighter.

"I don't know," Gabriel said. "I'm just . . ." He looked at his mask on the floor. The eye slits stared back at him, empty, dark. "I've got nothing."

All she did was raise an eyebrow.

"I'm not talking about you and me," he said. "I . . . this Axiom-man thing . . ."

"What? You want to quit?"

"No, no, no. Not that. I can't quit. Not with what's at stake."

"Which is?"

"Just . . . hang on a sec." He looked her in the face but not in the eyes. He didn't want any stern expression on his part to penetrate those eyes. The eyes that gave him hope. "I lost my job due to this stupid costume. I lost my home. I lost any means to support myself. I had to move in with you or be some sort of homeless vigilante. I don't even know what street etiquette is."

"Street etiquette? This is coming from the guy who spends his time immersed in this so-called 'street etiquette' and doesn't know what to do?"

Gabriel realized how he sounded. "No, I meant . . . just . . . . Is there a code for being homeless?"

"Okay, stop. A homeless code? Really?" She took a step toward him, firm. "You. Are. Not. Homeless."

"That's not what I . . ."

"Is this about money? You? Since when do you care about money?"

"Since I lost it." This was not going as planned. Not that Gabriel had a plan with this conversation but he didn't expect things to heat up.

She shot him a cold glare. "You don't care about money and you know it."

"That's not what I meant."

"You're here with me. You're safe. You're secure. None of your enemies know about us or where I live or anything like that. I'm working. I've got us covered."

Gabriel took in a slow breath but quickly exhaled. "Tonight, I saw an old man hand his wallet over to a mugger." He glanced to the floor. "I didn't follow up. Didn't restore the old man his wallet." He looked up at her. "The old man simply handed it over then used his *words* to make his point about the incident. His words, Valerie. He got the guy to think without using his fists."

"So?"

"Maybe I've been going about this all wrong?"

"Okay, look, I don't know what's wrong with you tonight but this isn't you. You've got something going on much deeper than an old man handing over his wallet or the missed opportunity to crack some teeth."

"Crack some teeth?"

"Punch the guy."

Gabriel closed his eyes a moment, pinched the bridge of his nose, and didn't like the feeling of the material of his glove touching his face. It'd be nice to just step out of the outfit and be himself. When he opened his eyes, Valerie had taken a step back. "I think it's all coming to a head."

"What is?" she said softly.

"This." He looked down at his costume, lifted a piece of his light blue cape. "Axiom-man."

"What makes you say that?"

"I've been doing this a while. I've made some headway dealing with these powers. I tried to use them for good. In the end, yeah, maybe I did, but this choice, this mission—it ruined my life."

"How? How does being able to save lives ruin a life?"

"That's not the angle I mean. I mean the personal toll. I don't know what I was thinking. I was just Gabriel Garrison, some random nobody working at a call centre. Then I meet the messenger and am suddenly thrust into a reality where ultra-powerful forces are at war, and I'm some kind of soldier assigned to lead the charge at the right time, but at the same stupid time, some dumb idiot out there gets almost the same powers and starts wrecking the place. He kills. No one stops him. He causes riots and the police to chase after petty criminals while he goes and conducts the—no, he *breaks* the law in big ways. Repeatedly. And it's not even about the law itself. Break it all you want. Some of society's rules are made-up garbage anyway. It's about the consequences, Valerie. Redsaw can rob a candy store or utterly tear a person apart and no matter what crime he chooses, lives are damaged and he causes a ripple effect throughout the criminal underworld, giving them confidence that if they screw up, if needed, he'd come and lay waste to whoever tries to stop them."

"Really. He said that. You know this."

Gabriel bowed his head. "No. I don't know this. I'm assuming. The point I'm trying to make is Redsaw has become more than some crazy killer with super powers; he's become an anchor point to all that is evil, and here I am, weaker than him, watching as he keeps causing trouble and killing people and nothing is being done."

"You're trying."

"Am I?"

"Aren't you?"

The question stung. If she was saying he hadn't been trying this whole time to stop Redsaw or wasn't trying in his efforts to clean up Redsaw's messes, then she was totally missing the point of what he was saying or, perhaps, he was doing a terrible job explaining it.

"You need to tell me what's wrong," she said good and firm. "If you're this upset and if we're talking about . . . powers . . . then this needs figuring out." She came up to him and took his fingers in hers. If only he could feel the warmth of her skin through his glove. "Wouldn't you agree?"

All Gabriel could do was nod.

"Now," she said, "let's start at the beginning and talk about what's really bothering you."

———

Another night of hookin' and another night of solid pay.

Jane's clients were high-end and she provided the experience. Nothing cheap. Nothing filthy. Just well-to-do hotels and clean sheets and a few client requests.

She glanced at the wad of cash wrapped in an elastic band at the bottom of her purse. There was over a thousand bucks sitting there. Not bad for four hours work.

She smiled at the chunk of bills, but when she looked up, the last thing she saw were glowing red fingers slicing across her neck.

———

"So, another murder. Same black cape. And, oh look, another one. Same black cape. And that one over there? Same *blue* cape. Why blue? Because the only weapon we have doesn't work!"

"Watch it, Gunn," Axiom-man said.

"No, *you* watch it." They were on top of City Hall, not on top of the precinct. Axiom-man had heard there was some shuffling in the police department and, as per the brief mentions in the papers, Jack Gunn was involved somehow. To what extent, he had a pretty good feeling he was about to find out.

Gunn took a step back and put his hands on his hips. He was a mess of a man, his head now nothing but gray, the hair several inches long and, to Axiom-man's surprise, a little bit wavy. Never pictured Gunn to be a guy with wavy hair. The man sported a long goatee that drew up into a shorter beard along his cheeks. Dishevelled clothes hung off his body and not for lack of weight. Jack Gunn was a hefty guy but didn't seem to have a clue about wardrobe. His brown-striped vintage button-down and worn gray pants under a large brown trench coat suggested all was bought at a thrift store. Axiom-man supposed Gunn was taking this whole disgruntled cop thing seriously and wanted to look the part.

"Do you have something to say?" Gunn said.

"What are you expecting?" He hated being up here with this guy. The way the moonlight caught Gunn's face made the man appear uglier than usual.

Gunn sighed then took a deep breath and a deliberate slow exhale. "Maybe I'm being too hard on you." The man said it so quietly Axiom-man hardly picked it up.

"I do the same to you."

Gunn took a step closer. "We've never gotten along, huh?"

"Not really," Axiom-man said. Then, after a pause, "Perhaps that's why we work so well together."

"Oh, don't get all sappy with me. Do you have any idea how dumb that statement sounds right now? Yeah, sure, you've saved the city a couple times. Yeah, sure, you help people out, bring some of the scum to me. But also, thanks to you, I've got some kind of shadow man sitting in a holding tank downstairs constantly talking about breaking out and covering not just the city but the entire country in darkness." Gunn looked down then back up. "After he kills you, of course."

"Of course." Axiom-man adjusted his cape. "Downstairs?"

"What, are you oblivious to everything's that gone on on the inside? And I'm not talking prison."

"The police?"

"Yes, the police. Why do you think we're on top of City Hall and not the station? Captain is done with this. All of it. The madness. The riots. The crime. The stupid idiots running around in tights and destroying everything. He's even done with you."

"He said that?"

"In short." Gunn scratched the top of his head, his fingers almost getting caught in the strands. Axiom-man wondered when the man last showered. "And the damn fool won't resign."

"Would he have to?"

"Not as long as he follows *his* job description, which is why he dumped everything on me, and by everything, I mean you looney tunes. The city's falling apart and we all know who's behind it."

"Redsaw."

"Thanks for joining the conversation. This one is on you, *Axiom*-man. You could have destroyed him when you had the chance. You were the one who fought him that night at the MTS Centre."

"Do you have any idea what went on—I mean *truly* went on—that night?" He thought about the Doorway of Darkness.

"Stop the vaguery."

Axiom-man debated telling him. Gunn might be temperamental and a douchebag, but he was a good cop and took the work seriously. Axiom-man doubted the man had anything else. Perhaps under different circumstances it would be an interesting conversation as to what drove him. "You're right." Gunn arched an eyebrow. "I didn't stop him. I couldn't. Not with everything that happened." *That was the night that tipped Valerie off I was Axiom-man.*

"I said stop with the vaguery. Of course things happened. Look around, Einstein. Do you think this is normal?"

"Have you ever watched the news reports from other countries? In those places, riots are normal."

Gunn, seemingly trying to save face, said, "This isn't about those places. This about a city burning down, a police captain who doesn't care and relocated everything from our Meta Defense Squad from the station to here."

"Meta Defense Squad?"

"I rebranded."

"Okay, so you're set up downstairs. How are you set up? What are you using?"

"That's just the problem. Captain wanted everything done in a jiffy so be damned with our equipment. Just pack it up fast and move it over. I still think a box or two is left at the station. Simply, we're not set up. Not like before. We had to get out so fast it was a scramble to gather everything and organize the muscle to carry it all over."

"Bleaken's cell?"

"Transportable. Designed that way in case he ever got close to getting out. The idea was we could try and get him somewhere remote so if he did break loose, it'd be a long haul back to the city to do whatever he would do."

"Okay, so a lot's happened. Got it. You can give me the nickel tour later."

"I wouldn't even do it for free. You're not wanted down there. Everyone working has taken it upon themselves to pick up after you because—" Gunn sucked in a deep breath and shouted, "You didn't stop Redsaw!"

Axiom-man knew Gunn was being unfair. He also knew Gunn was acting out of ignorance. This whole time, this whole thing with Redsaw, Axiom-man had kept most of what the battle was about to himself. Even Valerie didn't know all of it. But to tell Gunn what was really at stake? To tell Gunn Redsaw was probably making another attempt at opening the Doorway would drive the man into a frenzy, maybe even give him a heart attack. The messenger gave him his powers for a reason. The powers were, in large part, to stop Redsaw or a being like him. And Axiom-man knew deep down Redsaw served his own master. His own *messenger*. Or at least someone or some *thing*. He remembered when that black cloud first appeared above the city. He remembered flying and chasing it and how it made him feel ill when he got near it and how the same sick feeling came over him every time Redsaw was around. That cloud, whatever it represented or whatever it was, was no doubt what Redsaw served. *I can't tell Gunn. If I have to, I will, but not now. He's too wound up. He doesn't have the means to stop Redsaw. He doesn't fully understand the powers at play . . . and he has too much of an ego to be fine with staying in the dark if he knows there's something to discover.* Axiom-man clenched his jaw. "You're a good cop, Gunn."

"Well" —he scratched behind his ear— "I try, but these days I'm dropping the ball. Not enough manpower and boots on the street. Cops were never meant to handle an entire city all at once. There's no budget for that. Think about it: preserving peace for over eight hundred thousand people? What if all eight hundred thousand suddenly acted up and caused trouble? We'd be out manned in a bad way and we'd have to call the blasted army in to help. Know what cops are? A deterrent. Yes, there are good cops who put a lot of bad people away but do that math. Eight hundred thousand versus our force? Big problem. We can't even keep up with the riots and that's just the criminal fraternity. Can you imagine if others joined in because they had enough? Worse, if others followed their example? You know mob mentality? Dual-sided coin because sometimes it doesn't fall in the positive column and, sadly, it's also more prone to the negative side of things."

"Explaining to me the deficiencies of the city's finest only tells your boss you need help."

"And that's why we're up here, genius. We need to come up with a plan and you're our biggest gun."

Axiom-man thought about making the joke that between the two of them, Gunn was actually the bigger . . . gun. But he didn't. "What are you proposing?"

"For now, this is what I suggest: my guys are gonna sweep the streets as best as able and handle things they know they can handle for certain to at least take those items off the board. Second sweep will be slower because we're going after the harder guys to take down."

"Any third sweep?"

"Yeah. You. You're our third sweep, but you're going to do it while we work below. I need you to fly around and find that bastard before he causes any more trouble. If you see something below that's severe, get down there, fix it, then get back to looking for that lunatic in red. I hope you find him and I hope you find him quickly. Do whatever it takes to bring him down and bring him to me. Using lethal force is authorized."

"I won't kill."

"I said that once. Then I had to." Gunn's face was like stone.

Axiom-man looked him square in the eye. "I. Don't. Kill." He turned to fly away, but just before he did, he said, "I'll begin third sweep effective immediately."

"Take this." Gunn handed him a tiny comm unit. Axiom-man tucked it into his belt, making sure it was secure. "If you find him, let me know if you can stop him."

"If I find him, I'll put an end to this." Axiom-man turned, lifted his arms, and let his feet leave the roof but not before hearing Gunn mutter: "That's what they all say."

————

THE SUMMONING

And in those days the sun will turn to sackcloth and the moon to blood, Axiom-man thought. He knew the line just like most everybody else. Black and red. Just like Redsaw.

He kept himself flying just above the rooftops, close enough to the ground to see something happening, far enough away to hopefully go unnoticed so he could pursue Redsaw.

"Where are you hiding?" The man could be anywhere. Could be in any building. Could even be out of the city. Axiom-man doubted Redsaw was out here flying the streets.

But he couldn't leave that to chance.

A shrill scream caught his attention. It was hard to ignore but Gunn said to stick to the skies. *You're listening to Gunn now?* No. It was a strategic play. Gunn wouldn't let him see the Meta Defense Squad's headquarters which suggested it would be better for Gunn to take the lead for now. If he knew what the MDS was doing and was being truthful about it, then his assignment made sense. Axiom-man knew to listen to someone who might know more than him, so unless Gunn was covering up a huge police blunder moving the MDS, he had to trust that slob of a cop knew what was happening on the inside and that, for now, all was in hand. Gunn wasn't stupid and would call Axiom-man into the MDS if the situation warranted it despite what some people might say. Axiom-man knew if someone knew more than you did about something, it was best to listen until proven otherwise.

Ultimately, Gunn was right. This had to be a coordinated effort. Strategy. Outthink the enemy.

Unless your enemy out-thought you.

A billow of black smoke rose from the rooftops a couple blocks down.

Axiom-man headed toward it.

CHAPTER TWO

THE CLOSER AXIOM-MAN drew to the black smoke, the more his insides roiled. He knew this smoke. He knew this cloud. He remembered that night flying over the city and seeing a black cloud for the first time. He knew all too well the sickening sensation that rocked his insides when he got near it. But he had to endure. Had to force it.

Had to face it.

Axiom-man landed just on the peripheral of the black cloud. Even from here he wanted to throw up. *Ignore it. Keep it down. Imagine your body is reacting to something else, like bad take-out.* The thought didn't help but Axiom-man drew nearer to the black cloud anyway. With a rush of wind, the cloud quickly enveloped him and he found himself surrounded by sheer darkness.

His head swooned and his stomach flipped. He instinctively put a hand to his gut in an effort to contain what was within, which wasn't much: a quick grilled-cheese sandwich he made before taking to the skies.

Axiom-man lit up his eye beams in an attempt to use their light to help him see in the darkness. When Bleaken shrouded the city in shadow, using slight illumination from his eyes enabled him to see enough in the dark to find his way around. But now? It wasn't working. The thin layer of blue light covering his line of sight signalled his eyes were alit. Perhaps he had to turn up the power?

Axiom-man intensified the glow.

Still darkness outside of simply knowing his eyes were aglow.

"Bleaken?" Axiom-man said. "Step out."

THE SUMMONING

Silence.

Darkness.

The sickness alleviated but the darkness remained.

"Bleaken!" He didn't know how the man of shadow and cloud got out of his holding cell. Gunn made it sound like Bleaken was secure. "Bleaken!"

Nothing.

It was him. Had to be. Bleaken's clouds didn't make him ill. But what of his initial reaction to the clouds? Surely, there couldn't be two versions of it floating around the same spot.

Axiom-man put both hands to his stomach then tilted forward. He couldn't stay here, couldn't remain in the dark, couldn't—his head knocked to the side and it felt like his eyeballs spun like pool balls in corner pockets. Another quickly came in from the other side, resetting the spin and causing his head to go numb somewhere on the inside of his skull.

Axiom-man lashed out at the dark and struck nothing but black cloud. "Show yourself! Bleaken! Come on!"

Firm fingers wrapped themselves around either side of his ankles, gave a harsh tug, and pulled his legs out from under him. He landed hard on his chest and his chin smacked the roof.

With a feral scream, Axiom-man got on his knees, threw on the eye beams with force, blasting their rays into the darkness, aiming them right then middle then left, then in an arc like a rainbow from one side to the other.

He stopped.

"Hi." The voice was low. And near.

Axiom-man took a hard shot to the gut and doubled over. Another blow came down between his shoulder blades and sent him back to the rooftop. Grabbed by the material of his cape around the collar and one of his legs, he was hoisted up and spun in a circle before being tossed through the black cloud, out of it, and onto the rooftop. He skidded across the roof and only came to a halt when his back smacked into an air duct.

Battle Bruiser emerged from the cloud. The man was bigger than Axiom-man remembered but he still sported that dark, handle-bar mustache. The man's identity was concealed by a wide domino mask across his eyes. A heavy leather jacket adorned his muscular frame and thick-soled boots made each of his footfalls sound like thunder.

"You," Axiom-man said.

"That's right, blue boy. Come on," Battle Bruiser said with a wave of his fingers to come closer.

"How did you—" Axiom-man wanted to ask how Bruiser was able to see in the dark of the cloud not so much how he landed his shots, but before he could finish the question, Bruiser quickened his pace, came up to him, then drove his fist down hard alongside Axiom-man's cheekbone, forcing Axiom-man's head to face the rooftop.

"Okay," Axiom-man muttered. *No more.* He let Battle Bruiser get a bit closer, and just as the big man was about to pummel him with another blow, Axiom-man threw a wild uppercut and landed it square in the soft spot beneath Battle Bruiser's chin. *Stay on him. Like chopping down a tree.* Battle Bruiser straightened his head and glared at Axiom-man with cold eyes.

"You will regret—" the big man started but was cut short when Axiom-man clocked him hard across the head then kicked him in each of his knees with everything he had.

Bruiser's legs gave way beneath him. His knees hit the roof and he wiped a little blood off his chin. "Very good. This is much better than the last time we . . . talked."

It was a bigger fight last time in that electric cage, but back then, Axiom-man didn't know anything about Battle Bruiser or his strengths and weaknesses. With Bruiser, Axiom-man later figured out, the tactic had to be a simple one: brute force pinpointed at the right places. It was the only language Battle Bruiser understood, it seemed.

Axiom-man came down with another blow, this one aimed at the side of Battle Bruiser's neck. Bruiser caught his fist, halted its force, then pushed back. Axiom-man pushed toward him. He knew his fist wouldn't land even if he put on the ultra strength full force; the aim was off. But that was okay. Using his quasi-arm wrestle with Bruiser as a distraction, Axiom-man came in from the other side and sent the man's head torquing to the right.

A bone crunched. Or, at least, sounded like it did.

Bruiser slowly turned his head to face Axiom-man. Axiom-man aimed to hit him between the eyes, maybe blind him. As if that would help. If Bruiser could somehow make his way around in the dark smoke, then surely being temporarily blinded by a shot between the eyes wouldn't have an effect. Even still, Axiom-man had to try.

And he had to pull his punch or he'd punch *through* Battle Bruiser's head.

He let his fist fly and nailed Bruiser between the eyes. The big man's head snapped back. Axiom-man pounced on him and thrust his fist into Bruiser's teeth as the two went down. The man didn't react but blood spilled out of the corners of his mouth. Was he unconscious?

A strike to the side of Axiom-man's head knocked him off the big man. Bruiser? The man lay there but his arm moved, just adjusting.

Another shot.

How is he . . . ? He wanted to know how Bruiser was able to move his arm yet somehow connect a strike to the head. Did the man become telekinetic since they last fought?

Bruiser moved his arm again and flopped it over his chest. At the same time, Axiom-man received another blow to his shoulder, the force so hard he went numb right down the arm in vibrating shock.

"How?"

The hits came fast and hard and the black cloud rushed toward him with the low, almost guttural howl of an angry wind. A hit to his eye socket, another to this throat. One came in and struck the middle of his lower back, temporarily causing his legs to freeze.

Sick from the cloud, Axiom-man threw up inside his mask. He couldn't see Bruiser.

Something struck the back of his head.

He went down.

The cloud screeched.

CHAPTER THREE

AXIOM-MAN AWOKE TO find himself half-hanging over the ledge of the building, his arms dangling, just beyond his line of sight his gloved fingers pointing toward the street four or five stories below. The fabric of his mask still hugged his face and the sopping wet area of puke covered his mouth. He gagged. He hated throw-up. Couldn't stand the sight of it never mind actually doing it. His body weighed a ton and his ears rang. Slowly, he wormed his way back to safety on the other side of the ledge then, once slumped on the now cloud-free roof, he lifted the bottom of his mask, exposing his mouth to the night air so he could breathe better.

What's happening? He wasn't sure if the confusion was from the beating he just took or the possibility Battle Bruiser was stronger than their first encounter. That cloud weakened him so Bruiser could've been at the same power level as before but the cloud made the fight that much harder. Yet the cloud was also a mix of that which made him ill and that which didn't. Something wasn't right.

Gunn wanted him to seek out Redsaw and now look what happened.

Sirens rose on the street below and off in the instance, a mosaic of yellow, orange, and black rose from the street as something went up in flames.

With a groan, Axiom-man got to his feet and raced toward the fire. He flew at top speed at first, an urgent instinct to help taking over. Then he slowed his flight and hovered a few moments in the air. He took a good look at the smoke rising from the burning building and confirmed there was orange and yellow amidst it.

Better not be another black cloud disguised with flame.

Screams.

The people.

He flew over the fire. Flames engulfed a corner money mart type, the top two floors that sat above the outlet showcasing fire out the windows as if waving fiery curtains.

Axiom-man looked around for some water. A hydrant. A firetruck. Anything he could use to dowse the flames.

A man came running out of one the doors, arms flailing, his body engulfed in fire. He dropped to the street, screeching, rolling side to side, and even managed a crude summersault in an effort to suffocate the flames.

Axiom-man flew down, landed beside the man, then quickly draped his large cape over the fellow and patted him down. When nothing but gray smoke leaked from gaps in the fabric, he pulled his cape away only to reveal a smoldering corpse.

"Oh no . . ." he whispered. He knelt beside the body. The man's face was nothing more than fried, cratered skin, eyelids burned away, eyeballs bulging from a dead face. His clothes were mostly burned away, the plastics in some of the fabric having melted and glued themselves to his body.

For a moment, a sharp pang struck Axiom-man's heart at the loss, but within two seconds that hurt turned into rage and his heart swelled with anger. His face muscles tightened into a grimace . . . and he stood. Axiom-man tugged the bottom of his mask down and looked to the burning building.

There was nothing he could do about it. No resources to help. The best he could do was make sure anyone who might be inside were out and safe.

His feet left the ground and he got close to the building, the faint glowing aura around his body protecting him from the heat but not completely. He had to stay a good ten or so feet away from the flames otherwise he'd risk getting burned.

"Hey!" he shouted. "Anybody in there?" As if his voice was a trigger, the top floor came crashing down onto the one below. Flame and sparks and debris flew outward from the collision. Axiom-man distanced himself until things settled then got closer again. "Anybody—"

Glass broke below. Axiom-man didn't look and simply assumed it was a window blowing out.

Another window ejected a dark gray object in his peripheral. He looked down. It wasn't an object.

It was a person.

The gray person crouched over . . . something . . . acting like a mini wall that protected whatever it had as another shot of fire blasted out then receded. The gray person stood. From where Axiom-man hovered, it was difficult to tell if the person was male or female . . . but it didn't matter. What mattered was what they stepped away from—a child. From his vantage point, Axiom-man couldn't make out much about the kid but ballparked the little girl at around four or five, maybe six.

The person in gray stood still. The kid looked up at them as if seeking instruction. The person, at least from where Axiom-man was, didn't speak nor move. The kid slowly backed away.

Was this a kidnapping? The child appeared terrified.

The person still didn't move. What kind of person rescues a kid and then does . . . nothing?

The kid backed away, slow step by slow step, then took off in an all-out run to the east, disappearing down an alleyway.

Axiom-man flew after the kid to see if they were all right but when he got to the alleyway, the kid was gone.

Taking a deep breath then slowly exhaling, Axiom-man said softly, "Be careful."

He knew the feeling of being watched all too well but when he turned fully expecting to see the person in gray, they were gone as well.

"What?"

He looked up and down the street and every other way for them. There was no sign of them.

The building's fire took over the entire structure, crackling and roaring. The place was too demolished and aflame for anybody—even with his aid—to get out. Axiom-man just hoped that kid was the only one in there who needed out.

But that person in gray? A civilian? He hadn't been able to make out what they were wearing from his point of flight but noticed they concealed their head and face with a gray hood. He recalled some extra fabric over the figure but it could have been a baggy hoodie or something similar. Whoever they were, he was thankful they had the guts to go into the inferno and get the kid out.

And here you are having done nothing. Just get beat up, try to save someone who needs you only for someone else to do it for you. "Yeah, nice one, Gabriel."

He'd been out so many nights his internal clock was nearly in sync with the rising of the sun. Soon, this city would be in fiery chaos in broad daylight.

A couple squad cars zipped past on the street below, sirens blaring. He turned; on the opposite side an ambulance sped across the street.

What was happening? Where was the help? The army, maybe?

"Probably standing on the frontlines with their hockey sticks waiting for the fight to come to them," Axiom-man muttered. He thought Gunn was supposed to have a handle on assistance. *No, Gunn said the captain has pretty much turned his back on this. Well, turned his back on me. But surely the mayor would've made a call. Heck, even the Prime Minister would see what's going on and do something. He's leading this chunk of the continent after all.* "Or is everybody too scared to piss Redsaw off and risk hell?"

The thought gave him pause and, if anything, put the weight on his shoulders even more, so much so he drifted down a couple feet from where he hovered.

"It's all on me."

CHAPTER FOUR

OSCAR OWEN SAT at his vibrantly-polished wooden desk at his home office. The papers on the tabletop were a scatter of investment reports, planned projects, a few communications, and a box full of post-it notes.

Oscar's net worth was climbing. Rapidly. Every dollar and cent needed to be accounted for because he had no doubt an audit was in his future. It's one thing for a company to grow at a steady rate, quite another when revenues triple year over year.

But he knew what he was doing.

Insider trading, he thought, *with myself.*

The formula was easy: Anything Redsaw destroyed, offer to buy the property for a generous price to take it off the owner's hands and save them the headache of rebuilding. Then, once the land is obtained, clear out the rubble, put up a new structure, and make your money back and then some.

Yet, this wasn't about money. Money was a tool, nothing more. When Oscar first started on his strong financial path, yes, the money was exciting because he'd never seen so much before. There was a huge difference between a six-hundred-dollar paycheck pumping gas fulltime versus getting a notice your property value went up a hundred thousand dollars. But, after a while, after spending some of that cash and indulging in what it could provide—booze, women, lavish rooms and comfy beds—it was all old hat now. This was about something more than wealth. This was about the Doorway of Darkness.

THE SUMMONING

This was about reopening the door and letting his master through.

This was about showing the world what true power was, not some guy in a blue cape flying around and lifting heavy objects.

This was about changing the world.

Means to an end, he thought.

Putting Axiom-man in that electric cage with Battle Bruiser and Lady Fire was a good precursor for what was coming. Axiom-man had to be measured. It'd been a long enough while since he and Axiom-man tangled. He needed to know where his opponent stood and what he was capable of. If Axiom-man's powers functioned anything like his own, Oscar knew they were always in a state of flux, with power levels increasing without notice, sometimes by a lot, sometimes by a little, but ever-increasing nonetheless.

Axiom-man had stood his ground against Battle Bruiser and Lady Fire and put up a solid fight against two opponents. Two *superpowered* opponents. This indicated an increase in ability on Axiom-man's part and, like going into any business deal, you need to know who you were dealing with before executing any plans. That battle inside the electric cage, those rumblings of things to come, put Axiom-man on Oscar's chart as someone he had to be careful with. It was no secret Oscar could put on the black mask and demolish Axiom-man in an all-out fight . . . but he had lost to Axiom-man before on Black Saturday. Their first fight. Oscar's first loss. But he recalled that fight. It played on his mind nearly daily. It wasn't regret or reliving moments of woulda, coulda, shoulda—but rather a power analysis. The clashing of their energies and the purple energy stream that was created when their powers touched.

That purple stream. Part blue, part red. Part Axiom-man, part Redsaw.

Axiom-man had sealed the Doorway after it had taken Redsaw a plethora of nights of bloodshed to become strong enough to create it. It was no secret to the city he was doing the same thing now, that was, killing. The city just didn't know why and chalked him up as a lunatic and a serial killer with only one man able to stop him. It was so cliché it was laughable but at the same time, that's what it was.

Oscar was a boil-it-down kind of man. Show him the essence of what the goal is then break it down into pieces to be tackled one at a time for the endgame.

His latest realty acquisitions. One of the pieces. Each property, a beacon to enhance his power to reopen the Doorway.

Oscar thought back to that purple stream. *Axiom-man closed the Doorway with his power. I opened it with mine. If he and I were to open it together, to somehow get him to exert his power upon the door as I try to open it—that mix might disrupt the seal, confuse it, loosen it.* Or, alternatively, reinforce the seal to a certain extent or weaken it because the purple stream would contain some of Axiom-man's power. "The only way for that idea to possibly work is based on the premise the Doorway is like a machine: throw a wrench in and a problem is inevitable. But it's a gamble given the possible alternatives."

He didn't know what he was going to do. He just knew what had to be done and a few of the steps to get there.

Step one: Fear. In Axiom-man. Showing him those he stopped before are now back for revenge. Make him the hunted. Make him pay.

THE SUMMONING

Show him, with each blow from his enemies, that Redsaw oversaw all.

———

Gabriel stood in the shower facing away from the hot water running over his back. Face in his hands, heart thumping hard and steady, he made an effort to breathe in and out slowly. Just enjoy the warmth, breathe, slow down.

"You're making too much of a deal out of this," he whispered into his palms. "What? Did you think you could do what you do and not make any enemies? No, you already knew that. You knew that from Day One which is why you wear the mask, outside of attempting to be some kind of symbol, an axiom of truth and goodness and kindness." He listened for Valerie in the other room but couldn't hear anything past the pouring water and the bathroom fan. But he knew she was there, somewhere, outside the bathroom door, here, under the same roof. "You can't lean on her too hard. She's already concerned and you can tell she's worried about you. She cares about you and about what you do as Axiom-man." He breathed in deep then exhaled. Some of the water pooled on his palm rippled from the exhale. "Don't drag her into this too far. Keep her on the outside where she's safe." If Redsaw found out who he was, Valerie would no doubt be in his sights. Heck, if any of his enemies knew who he was, Valerie and his family would be the first ones attacked. "Thank goodness for the mask," he breathed into his hand. *But the mask is the problem. It was intended for good. You even got rewarded for making the choice. You've gotten surges and commendation. But is this how it will go? Keep doing good, keep getting more power, keep putting people at risk—more and more powerful people coming? More powerful than Redsaw?*

This whole thing, this whole battle of power, it all started when Redsaw showed up. All started with that black cloud. If Redsaw hadn't shown up or if that cloud hadn't shown up—if he hadn't received his powers from the messenger, perhaps all this could have been avoided. Life was life before that night of visitation. The world, though full of turmoil and political injustice, ran on in what folks considered a more or less normal state.

Then otherworldly power was introduced to planet Earth and, quickly after, *more* unearthly power.

Gabriel decided the natural order of things had been upset and turned around.

Him first.

Redsaw second.

Everybody else third.

He turned and faced the stream of water and let it rinse his face. He ran his hands back over his hair, getting it out of his eyes, then turned around again. "I'm not supposed to be here. *Axiom-man* is not supposed to be here. The messenger made a mistake," he whispered. "No, he told you why you were picked. You were the last one genetically able to handle the gift. It was you or nobody. Or, you or anybody else with the same genetic markers. You weren't picked because of outstanding morals or good behavior. You were picked because there wasn't a choice." *Or was there? The messenger is powerful. Could he not have somehow changed somebody else to have been able to accept the gift? Or is that beyond his scope?*

All Gabriel knew at that moment was what was done was done. Perhaps after dealing with a city gone to hell and some people with powers they shouldn't have, perhaps after figuring out a way to banish them from the Earth, the natural order of things could be restored?

Perhaps, when this was all over, the blue cape could be hung up for good.

If Gabriel felt he could let the crusade go, that was.

He turned the water off, gave himself a mild shake, then pulled back the curtain and stared at the heap of bright and dark blue material on the floor.

He stared at the suit for a long time. He wasn't really looking *at* the suit but at the same time, each fold in the fabric, each bunch of material, the bundle of partly-rolled-up cape on the floor—it needed him.

And he needed it.

Redsaw still haunted the streets.

CHAPTER FIVE

A BLAST OF red energy ripped across the mannequin display windows along the side of the old Hudson Bay building downtown. A combination of heated and cool glass sprayed outward in a rain shower of crystal; the once-adorned-with-the-latest-fashion naked mannequins went up in flames along with their surrounding walls in the tight space.

Quickly, that same blast of red energy ran along the height of the building, bottom to top, setting one of Canada's oldest former retail outlets ablaze.

The Hudson Bay dated back to the trading era where the Red River met the Assiniboine at the Forks. Its building downtown was all that was left of an era long gone.

Redsaw grinned then took off into the sky.

All it takes is a little panic and these fools don't know what to do with themselves. Humans were predictable and, at their core, animals with instincts. Redsaw knew the power of the mind and how it could be used to override any logical response with a little practice. But these humans didn't understand that.

He paused his flight mid-air and hovered. "Am I human anymore?" Humans didn't bear the gift of the gods. And if they did, as per the multiple legends throughout the world, then they certainly were not your average human being. At minimum, they were a hybrid of human fragility and superhuman power. "And gods rule and have supreme authority," he said. Supreme authority was something he knew he lacked. If he was an intended supreme being, he wouldn't have to answer to his master and, right now, his master wanted out of the realm behind the Doorway of Darkness. To what end, his master never revealed.

Complete and utter rule would've been Redsaw's guess.

Then that leaves me where? He'd already surpassed the odds by building an empire from the ground up. He went from rags to riches simply by starting small and taking a chance. Increasing human power and ability became easier and easier the farther up the societal ladder he climbed. Once you had resources, it was easy to turn them into more resources and multiply assets and extend further and further reach into the affairs of the human world. It had been told to him long ago his master assisted him in what he needed, working from behind the curtain, pulling strings where and when needed, exalting Redsaw higher and higher in the human realm.

"He wants to give influence from the inside, not just the—" It suddenly became clear. His master was being thorough by intent: infiltrate human society from the inside via the channel that was Oscar Owen and exert power to tear worldwide systems down, one by one. *I will not be a pawn!* Additional pressure from Redsaw only ensured further control.

Destruction within, destruction on the outside.

A human would crumble.

The chaos in the city proved that. These people, whether they realized it or not, were being squeezed internally *and* externally. Anybody would crack.

Except, Redsaw knew, he wouldn't. He had a foot in each world, both natural and metahuman. He saw—and *was*—both sides of the coin.

His heart sunk at the prospect of what might happen should his master be fully unleashed. Would there be a use for him after the fact? Would he become some sort of soldier—perhaps the *only* soldier—to be dispatched when needed to keep the humans in subjugation?

Redsaw knew this feeling. He had lost control. Worse, he might never have had control to begin with. His master gave him his power, his master had a hand in his earthly endeavors, his master was calling to him from behind the Doorway.

He—it—needs me. I'm here. He's over there. Trapped. He grimaced. The words were more than a thought; they echoed in his heart. For now, he had to let the master use him if he was to see where all this would ultimately end. He had to let the master use him to potentially grow in power and achieve a level of strength that would indeed put him on the level of godhood. Some sort of transformation that would remove whatever parts of Oscar Owen that were left in him and become Redsaw through and through.

This was about outthinking his master.

Redsaw shook inside, glanced past his black boots to the street far below and the orange glow of the fires casting a dusk-like ambience on the city. He wasn't ready to challenge his master. He didn't even know the extent of his master's power. It must be vast if he had to stay on the other side of the Doorway. Was that world of red and black a place of condemnation or a place of absorbing power?

I can't challenge him. You don't go into something like this without knowing your opponent. Really knowing them. Can he hear my thoughts? He immediately silenced his mind, washed out any lingering pondering on what he was just thinking and decided he'd go step by step lest he risk losing it all, both as Oscar Owen but, worse, as Redsaw.

He could not let his power go.

THE SUMMONING

He would die first.

———

"Are you there?" Gabriel asked the dark.

He was in the bathroom, the only place he was sure Valerie wouldn't walk in on him. He activated his powers, a thin film of blue light over his vision. "I could really use your help."

Gabriel needed the messenger, but the messenger did not answer him on Gabriel's terms but on his own.

"Seems like everything that's happened up until now is coming to a head," Gabriel whispered. "I can't find Redsaw and he's destroying the city. I can't stop him unless I find him." He shuddered at the thought of facing Redsaw again. As much as he was confident his powers would see him through, he also knew from past encounters Redsaw always seemed to have an edge on him. He just hoped the recent surges in his abilities were enough to overpower Redsaw once and for all. This also meant an inevitable fight with inevitable pain.

"If you could just show up for once when I need you, give me some reassurance, some sort of . . . I don't know . . . something to let me know all this will be okay."

The dark responded with nothing, and Gabriel wasn't surprised. The energy over his eyes grew brighter and crackled. Why did the messenger always leave everything up to him?

"Because you were trusted with these powers and it's your choice how you use them," he reminded himself with the slight suggestion of a feeling he wasn't saying those words alone. Perhaps the messenger was prompting the reminder.

Was that you?

The dark of the bathroom immediately felt cold and the unsettling feeling of true loneliness crept in.

Gabriel powered down and let the black of the dark de-stimulate his eyes and the silence bring comforting quiet to his ears.

"You're out there," he whispered. "I'm not doing this anymore. You've wrecked my life from the start. You've been a constant threat to this city. You're a danger to people worldwide. You. Are. Evil."

Gabriel let his power swell within and burst forth.

He was going to find Redsaw, and he was going to find him now.

Chapter Six

Valerie checked her hair in the mirror. It was getting a little long for her liking but the advantage she found to the length was it made the loose ringlets drape appealingly over her shoulders.

Gabriel hadn't come home last night and he wasn't home now.

She put on a light layer of rose-red lipstick, double-checked her eyelashes for any excess makeup, then ran her hands smoothly down her hips over her black skirt. The blouse—dark blue—was a little too dressy for work today but at the same time, dressing up a little nicer than usual for work never hurt anybody.

This job had changed her life. The transition from working at Dolla-card to working for Mr. Owen wasn't a hard change in terms of action, but it certainly was a transition in terms of pay. Not that she was making money hand over fist working for Mr. Owen, but compared to Dolla-card, her salary was a little over one and a half times her previous earnings and, for her right now, she had more money than she knew what to do with. She was so used to living on her Dolla-card salary this bump in pay made her wonder what her next move would be. She would have to be smart about it. Too many in her extended family had come into some extra funds, and instead of doing something worthwhile, they squandered it on nonsense like an upgraded bottle of whiskey or a whole new wardrobe solely because the means were there versus actually needing new clothes.

Whatever. She had to put it out of her head for now. It was time to go to work.

She left the bathroom, flicked off the light, then walked past the bed and glanced at Gabriel's side.

In all truth, Valerie wasn't sure if he'd be coming home today. She just hoped, at some point, he'd come in and rest.

Even Axiom-man had limits.

———

The morning sunlight was not welcome. Axiom-man had to squint against its shine and the corners of his eyes ached after flying around the city all night. He kept to the skies as best as able but every so often had to go street level to help someone or stop a group of crazies from robbing or tearing down a place.

The fatigue forced him to stop his flight and settle on a nearby rooftop. He put one foot up on the ledge, the other remaining on the roof proper. Axiom-man looked both across the rooftops and along the streets below.

There was no sign of Redsaw.

Okay, stop, think. It took a moment for his tired mind to continue the thought flow. *Every encounter with Redsaw has always been about muscle versus muscle. Sure, there were a few other items at play but ultimately it came down to a fight.* His heart sunk into his stomach. He *hated* fighting Redsaw. Not only was his opponent stronger than him, the very presence of the man caused something to twist and turn within his powers, making him feel ill. Hard to fight when your body is screaming to lie down. The only thing Axiom-man had been able to do in the past to withstand that feeling while still putting up a fight was just sheer adrenaline and determination. Block the acknowledgment of feeling like garbage so it's out of your mind and all that mattered was the task at hand.

THE SUMMONING

It's been a thinking game from the start. You idiot! You've been going about fighting Redsaw wrong all this time. He knows he's more powerful than you so that means every time we fought, I either had the will to face him despite being out gunned, or he's been toying with me every time. He could've been pulling his punches for all I know. Not that those punches didn't hurt. They did. A lot. But perhaps Redsaw wasn't offering full aggression with each strike. Or maybe he was and Axiom-man was overthinking this whole thing. His brain power was already nearly tapped out. He needed a bed, some PJs, and a long sleep without all this stuff weighing on his mind.

"You're still going to have to outthink him," Axiom-man said quietly. A pigeon fluttered down and landed near him. "Did you see him?" The pigeon pecked at the rooftop, seeming to snatch up a tiny something only it noticed. "Didn't think so." He watched the pigeon. "What do you do when you want something but can't figure out how to get it?" The pigeon looked at him for a brief moment then rustled its wings. "I don't know even know how smart you are. For a pigeon, I mean. You obviously have to problem-solve on a daily basis to survive." *You search for food, evade predators, maybe get a little exercise in, possibly visit with other pigeons.* "You're not functioning one hundred percent on pure instinct. Yeah, instinct probably tells you what to do but surely you've got to work things out mentally now and then to make it day by day." He sighed. "And . . . you're talking to a pigeon." The pigeon turned its tiny head toward him as if it knew he was talking about it. "Do you have a name? I mean, some sort of pigeon name? Or do you guys just all acknowledge each other as fellow pigeons and that's it?" He was segueing, which meant he was fumbling for answers. Bad habit. Stop. Stay on target.

Outthink Redsaw.

"No," Axiom-man said. "Though trying to stay one step ahead is going to be a part of this, I can't let the thoughts get tangled as I try to come up with a solution." *Okay, break it down. Keep it simple. Nuts-and-bolts it. Redsaw is causing riots and chaos. He's out there. So is Battle Bruiser. That's two. Set aside. Next. Redsaw can't be physically located as per my efforts. Sucks, but fact for now so acknowledged. Battle Bruiser did make himself known, gave me a beating, and is still at large. Fine. Set that side. Next. Battle Bruiser is basically a bulldozer and slugs his way through stuff. A threat and a danger, yes, but compared to Redsaw, he's secondary. Noted. Set aside. Next. Redsaw is purposefully evading you but not out of fear. If he was afraid, he wouldn't be out there doing what he's doing. So again, he's playing with you. What's his endgame?* It was obvious: *kill me.*

"That's too simple," Axiom-man said. "Think harder. Review. Evaluate. Slow down. You're tired. Rooftop secure except for Mr. Pigeon who may or may not be a spy." He cracked a wry smile then his face relaxed beneath his mask before realization hit: *Redsaw is afraid of you.* The realization made him stop breathing and only when he coughed did he realize he'd been holding his breath. "He could've taken you out whenever he wanted but he didn't. Yeah, he might be toying with me, but unless there's more to his plan outside of being the dominant force for evil in this city—maybe worse—taking me down for good would have been the smart choice because then he'd have free reign. Lots you could do without someone being a check to your actions along the way."

Battle Bruiser was a distraction and someone to take me down a peg or two. He recalled the strike he received and the pain and spaciness after. He shook off the unsettling feeling. His mind went blank but not for being stuck on thinking this through. An idea began to form—*He's dividing and conquering. He's using the oldest—but very effective—technique in the book. Not only is he messing up the city, he's dividing me against me, making my inside and what's going on outside fight against each other. He's purposefully leaving you alone but still letting you know he's there. He's wanting your head to break down so your body—your powers—can follow. He's trying to mentally back me into a corner.* His facial muscles tightened and a second later, a grimace formed. "You're hiding. You're letting Time do its work. And you'll wait it out until you're sure you can attack full force and without hindrance." *If you've been anything throughout all this, it's patient. A good quality but with bad intentions.*

What felt like a brick of lead eased off Axiom-man's heart and he felt lighter. "You're in one of these buildings, you bas—" Sirens rose on the air. Axiom-man searched the streets below. Wherever the droning alarm came from, it was not from the streets within his line of view.

"Stick to the skies. Let Gunn handle the streets."

And this time, "sticking to the skies" became a metaphor.

He knew what he had to do to find Redsaw.

And it was going to cause trouble.

CHAPTER SEVEN

OSCAR CAME UP to Valerie's desk, put one hand on it, the other holding a couple of manilla file folders. He stared at the folders but didn't say or do anything with them.

Valerie noticed her boss had been a little out of sorts these past few weeks and, today, the gray shadow under his eyes made his black hair look darker, his visage slightly haunting. Whatever the man was going through, it was clearly keeping him up at night.

"Mr. Owen?" she said. His gaze was still lost in the folders. "Um, Mr. Owen?"

"Yes, Valerie. Sorry. Drifted off for a second there."

"Are you okay?"

He paused and then offered a faux smile, one she saw right through. "Yes, fine," he said. He passed her the folders. "I'm done with these. Please file them but mark the top one with a sticky with a big asterisk on it."

"Sure," she said. She searched her desk for a pad of sticky notes.

Oscar lingered at her desk.

"Is there anything else you need?" Valerie asked. "Coffee? You look tired."

He gave her a knowing smile. "I'm always tired, but that's not an excuse for not getting anything done." He winked. "Born and raised by parents who were born and raised by parents from, as they call it, the old country." He nodded slightly to himself and gave a soft chuckle. Valerie raised an eyebrow. Mr. Owen was never one for non-work-related chitchat. He looked her in the eye. "Two excuses for not getting something done: You're either so sick you can't move or you're dead. Those were the options I was raised with otherwise it was go to school, go to work, how you felt be damned."

"That sounds . . . harsh." While her own parents had been fairly strict, they never forced her to be a machine. Maybe it was Mr. Owen's upbringing in terms of work ethic that got him to where he was?

"Harsh. Unfair. Zero consideration for how a person truly feels. Again, old country. If we are to call our grandparents anything, it's they were hard workers even to the point of detriment. They never learned balance, but during their time, balance wasn't really an option. Forced from homes during World War II, never mind going through whatever they went through to get to the other side and survive. Rebuild from nothing. Makes total sense why they'd strive night and day to reestablish a life."

"Never thought about it that way."

"Point is, Valerie, you don't get anywhere by not doing anything. You can think and dream all you want, and while thoughts and dreams are where things start, if you let them stay that way, that's all they'll ever be." He maintained eye contact and leaned in a little closer. Valerie stirred in her seat. The shadows under his eyes were . . . disturbing . . . and were so out of place for a man who usually was business suave at all times. "But if you act—failure or success—then they are no longer thoughts and dreams, are they? It's alchemy: Turning the intangible into the tangible." He cracked a small grin. "Modern day magic."

"Yeah, well, magic seems to be a part of the norm these days."

"How so?" He seemed genuinely curious as to what she was about to say.

"Just meaning that relatively recently—compared to the rest of history, I mean—our world has gone from one of natural occurrences to one of—"

He finished for her. "Unnatural occurrences."

"And people."

"And people," he said. "What you do think, Valerie? I know what you're talking about. Do you think those 'special' people out there are unnatural?"

She had to watch what she was about to say. She had to protect Gabriel and any inkling of his true identity. "If you want to be utterly objective and call a spade a spade, then the answer is yes."

"That black and white?"

"It was a black-and-white question."

Oscar went silent and Valerie thought she had spoken out of turn. Then he said, "It was. But there's always plenty of room for gray."

––––––––

Axiom-man gave his head a shake in an attempt to wake up. It worked for all of ten seconds then the fatigued returned. He wasn't all-out exhausted but he was getting there. He needed sleep. A solid eight or nine hours to recharge. The issue was during those eight or nine hours, that was a decent part of the day when Redsaw could wreak more havoc, and it'd be Axiom-man's fault for what was basically sleeping on the job. This was the only part of being a world-proclaimed superhero he didn't like: the expectation to carry on without consideration for how he might be feeling. But that was part of the sacrifice of the cape. The world looked at him one way and it was not the way he looked at himself. He couldn't blame how he was viewed. He had no choice but to put up the front of the never-tiring hero. It was one of the only ways to instill hope. People needed to know someone was there for them twenty-four-seven, no different than making an emergency medical call in the middle of the night and knowing someone was available to help in the capacity needed.

The sooner you find him, the better. He glanced to the sky. The morning light muted the glow of the fires and amplified the darkness of the smoke. Axiom-man didn't want to do it. He hated talking to Gunn, but Jack Gunn was his only dependable ally in all this. He pulled the miniature comm unit Gunn gave him from his belt.

He pressed the tiny button on the side of the unit. "Gunn, are you there?"

Silence.

Probably passed out over a desk with a smoldering cigar beside him.

When Gunn came on the comm, it did indeed sound like he'd been sleeping, a voice full of gravel. "Better be good."

"No. Nothing good."

"I told you to—"

"You're not ordering me around and I'm not having this discussion right now. I'm giving you a heads up. You want Redsaw found, I have an idea, but I'm going to need to cause some trouble to get it done."

"Trouble? What kind of trouble?"

"The kind that's going to make your superiors hate me even more."

———

Axiom-man flew by Valerie's window at work. She immediately bolted from her chair to get a glimpse of

Gabriel. She wasn't sure what had become of him last night or where he had gone. Though a quick streak of blue flying by was enough to let her know he was safe.

"Finish it," she said quietly. Face firm, she turned from the window and went back to her seat.

———

The difficult part about locating Redsaw was the smoke that drifted up from various places across the city. The dark smoke of burning plastic and rubber from the riots made their clouds hard to discern between the black clouds of importance. Axiom-man kept his eyes sharp, fought back the fatigue that made them want to close, and focused on the gradients between the clouds, searching for the darkest one.

The blackest one.

He stopped mid-flight then realized he was going about it wrong. Seeking out the black clouds was one thing, but the possibility of triggering a portal was another and this was no time to be sucked into another world or, perhaps, for someone dangerous to come through due to an accidental action on his part. But they were tell-tale signs of Redsaw.

I wish I knew who he really was, Axiom-man thought. *It would make this so much easier. Yeah. Good one. Wishful thinking.*

He headed south toward the older part of Winnipeg. If there were any rundown or abandoned buildings, those would be there.

It was time.

Axiom-man kicked on the speed, revving himself up to over one hundred kilometres an hour. He focused and brought his forearms criss-crossed in front of his face but not so high as to cover his line of sight. He focused hard on his aura, hoping his concentration would gather it up and more thickly engulf his arms. His forearms and fists didn't glow any brighter despite the effort but that didn't necessarily mean it wasn't working. It took a lot to power up to the point where the glow was amplified.

Axiom-man let the blue energy build up in his eyes, coating his vision in a haze of bright blue. This, he knew, he was good at. Lots of practice heightening and lowering their power since receiving the ability. He brought things up to about a three-quarter charge.

This was either going to hurt or his aura would absorb most of the blow.

"I'm sorry, Winnipeg," he said, then drilled forward, blasting through the bottom windows of the first abandoned building he saw. Once inside, he took a quick scan to ensure no one was on the lower level. *Think practically.* Due to the severe momentum of moving at such a high speed, changing course required him to dig deep into his ultra strength to maneuver.

He took out the first support pillar he saw, sending it up in a coarse shatter of large chunks of cement and steel. He grunted as he forced his body to circle around and head straight up through the thick wood to the second floor. This floor was also clear. Axiom-man headed straight for what he presumed was the loading-bearing wall on this level and smashed through the other side into the smoky air. Without delay, he double back, striking the third and final floor, crashing through the brick, quickly reviewing the coast was clear, then again straight through the dense wall on the other side. With one final loop in the air, turning him back toward the building, he aimed for the bottom floor again and drilled through the support pillar opposite the one he just destroyed. Without breaking speed, he cleared the debris, smashed through the wall, flew about fifty feet away then spun mid-air and stopped to watch.

The building stood silent. Firm. The only thing different about it was the holes he had punched through the walls.

Disappointment began to settle in his heart and just as he was about to plow into the building again, he stopped himself when the building buckled, the lower floor dropping a foot. Three seconds later, the top floor collapsed, slamming down on top of the second, its weight driving the second floor down to the first, the disabled support pillars now no stronger than a coat hanger. The whole thing came down on top of itself in a violent spray of dust and rubble.

Axiom-man waited. If Redsaw was inside, and unless he was purposefully playing the possum card, he should emerge any moment, if indeed he was here.

Axiom-man waited almost ten minutes for him to arise out of the rubble. He didn't. The only things that arose were sirens on the air, no doubt in response to whomever phoned in the destruction.

Axiom-man turned in the air and headed for the next abandoned building. Doing the same thing, arms up and charged, eyes powered and ready, he piled on the speed and this time smashed through the half-broken windows of the top floor, scanned for life, found none, smashed through the window on the other side then circled back and did the same for the floor beneath that one and the floor beneath that.

All clear.

Bottom floor. Four obvious metal support pillars with probably a few hidden ones encased in concrete. Flying through, Axiom-man unleashed the beams from his eyes, obliterating one of the pillars. He crashed through another, his aura absorbing most of the blow but his forearms still ached to his bones from the impact. With a growl, he sent forth another round of energy beams and took out another pillar before swiftly exiting the building, and just in time too, because this one collapsed the second he was out. Dust and debris and brick and concrete and steel shot outward.

Like before, Axiom-man waited.

No Redsaw.

"If I have to, I'll tear this city a part to find you."

CHAPTER EIGHT

OSCAR OWEN LOOKED out the window from his top-floor office. He could see everything from here. Of course, he could see even more when he was in the sky, but right now, what he saw was enough: A city on fire.

The news was on: *"Axiom-man is on a rampage throughout the city. What he's doing or why, nobody knows, but he's leaving nothing but destruction in his wake. God only knows how many lives are at risk because of what he's doing."*

"What *are* you doing?" Oscar said quietly. He folded his hands behind his back and furrowed his brow. "I know you well enough to know this is on purpose." He paused and though the next words from his mouth caused him discomfort, he couldn't deny it was true. "You're making yourself look as bad as me."

Had Axiom-man snapped? Had Oscar finally gotten him to the point of driving him mad and making him careless? Or was this all a carefully calculated move to draw him out?

"I'm not coming," Oscar said. "Not when you're acting crazy."

Observe, think, act, he thought.

It was time Axiom-man came to an end.

———

Five empty buildings had already gone down. No Redsaw.

Come on, you have to be somewhere, Axiom-man thought. The comm unit in his belt beeped loud and clear, over and over again. Clearly Gunn was pissed. *"Stick to the skies," he said.* He knew Gunn hated it when orders were disobeyed. Thankfully, he didn't answer to Gunn. He answered to no one except the messenger. If Axiom-man was being honest with himself, he didn't like the idea of being his own authority especially since he was raised under strict authority then submitted to authority—that was certainly exercised—when at work. He answered to Valerie for some things due to their relationship, but ultimately there was no man or woman on the planet who could act in an authoritative capacity toward him. Not even Redsaw.

"Messenger, if you can hear me, I'm doing this for the good of everyone despite what it might cost."

Twenty minutes later, three more buildings had come down.

Somehow Gunn was able to shout through the comm without Axiom-man pressing the button. Perhaps there was an override of some kind. "Are you crazy! Get back here now! You're going to jail. A big jail with big bars and lots of hard time and lots of people around you who hate you and will kill you! Get your as—"

Axiom-man turned off the comm. Completely. Gunn was in no position to be of pragmatic help at the moment. Nothing but temper and rage.

Axiom-man dove down, arms crossed in front of him, and slammed through the roof of another building, this one only a couple storeys. He glanced across the second floor of the warehouse to ensure no one was inside then crashed through the ceiling of the first floor and did a wild circle around the square room, taking out all the support pillars.

He exited. The building came down.

"Redsaw!" he screamed into the air.

There were plenty of more buildings to go, and Axiom-man would not stop until that man in the black mask and cape was found . . .

. . . before Axiom-man's sanity was completely lost.

———

This was nuts!

Oscar could only grin. Finally, he had broken Axiom-man. No rational human being would go around destroying parts of the city unless there was something wrong with them.

But is he human? Oscar still did not know even after all this time. The logic said yes, but that was solely based on the fact that, thus far, no extra-terrestrial had made itself known on the planet.

Yet that still didn't mean some might be in hiding or, if Axiom-man was alien, it was possible just one of them made themselves public.

It doesn't matter, alien or not. I know his power. I know him. He took a deep breath. *That's only partially true. Redsaw knows him. I know him . . . but I don't know who lurks beneath that blue mask.* "But would it make a difference?" he said quietly, taking a quick note of his reflection in the glass. The man he saw was certainly not Redsaw. There was no indication in his appearance that he and Redsaw were one and the same. *And I know the same is true for you, my blue friend. Whoever you are, you blend in when not wearing that cape. You walk among us, carrying with you nothing but self-righteousness and cynicism over the behavior of mankind. You judge. You act. You have freedom from restraint, if you choose.* "But I think the cuffs are off." Way off in his line of sight, a plume of dust burst up high into the air. Another building. "You've lost control."

THE SUMMONING

A hint of pressure pressed against his esophagus and his head went light. Something pushed gently against the side of his head, tilting it toward the right. The black around his vision and the low ringing in his ears signaled somebody had him, somebody quiet, somebody . . .

———

The room was tiled a grimy beige, the grout missing in places, crumbling in others. One lone one-foot-by-two window was high up on the wall to the right, the light coming through muted from what were probably gray clouds.

Oscar peered left then right. Just beige walls with spatters of dirt and smears of something oily. Black still rimming his vision like a pair of glasses, he glanced down at his feet. His ankles! Each ankle was tied to a thick, rusty metal chair leg with some sort of clearly evident expert sailor's knot. The floor was cement and rough, cracks running along its surface.

The black around his vision disappeared and any lingering blur of the room cleared. Pressure on his wrists and around his fingers. He couldn't see them. They were tied to the chair behind his back so tight there was no option to bring them around. His hands were balled into fists with something coating them. He tried wriggling his fingers, tried to expand them. He couldn't. A quick mental flash of duct tape binding his fingers and hands so he couldn't use them skipped across his mind. And those were definitely ropes on his wrists. The rough, prickly texture told him it was the same rope that bound his ankles. Oddly, his mouth wasn't gagged or covered. Whoever did this wanted him to be able to talk.

He tried to stand, see if it was possible to get on his feet and duck-walk around the room in an effort to find something to free himself.

They don't know who they've got. He was about to ignite the red energy in his hands to escape his bonds but upon an absentminded glance upward, he saw a security camera in each corner of the room. If he used his powers, he'd give himself away if those cameras were on and the little red light near the lens indicated they were. *Clever.* The thought was more for himself. Either whoever had him knew he was Redsaw and was just waiting to catch something fantastic on camera, or they didn't know who he was and were simply keeping tabs.

It was possible that—

A sharp jolt of penetrating pain shot through his skull from behind, the strike getting him right where his skull met his vertebrae. It was enough to send his head down and forward so hard his chin banged into the top of his collarbone.

The room spun and for a moment and Oscar forgot where he was. When he came back around, the echo of the strike still rang through his head. *Unleash and kill.* His powers begged to be let out. He'd ignite his hands, use his strength to free his feet, stand, and obliterate whoever was in the room with him. Wait. Was there someone? He listened for breathing, movement, anything.

All was quiet.

Another strike sent his head forward again. This time when he was coherent enough to observe the room, the tops of dark gray boots filled his vision.

———

THE SUMMONING

As Axiom-man flew across the building tops, the sirens below kept their sound near, meaning the cops below were following his flight pattern via their squad cars.

*Now I'm the villain. Gunn is pissed, so pissed he seems to have diverted attention needed on the streets to me. That's not how it's done. I know what I'm doing. I know what I'm thinking. I know what I'm planning. I know what I—*His heart sank.

He didn't know what he was doing.

Sure, he *knew* his actions, but the motive was starting to slip on him. This was about finding Redsaw. This was about ending his reign of terror. This was about putting to rest a cosmic battle that most on the Earth didn't know was raging. This was about—

Axiom-man paused flight then landed on a rooftop. The accompanying sirens below told him the boys in blue were waiting for him at street level. It'd only be a matter of moments before the bullhorn came out and someone was shouting at him. Possibly even Gunn.

"He's winning," Axiom-man said quietly. "Look what he's making you do." Rage and sadness filled him to the point where his stomach swam. "You're being played. Deliberately or not, I don't know, but either way, you're falling." He paused. "And you're failing." *Valerie. If this stuff is making the news, which it no doubt is, and she's paying attention, she's gonna think I lost it. As smart as she is, I don't think she'll get this. There is no anchoring point to relate to.* A sharp pang struck his heart. *I could lose her.*

"You're not," he said, his voice a rasp. He glanced out over the city.

He needed to find out who Redsaw was.

Chapter Nine

"PHILIPPINES. POKER. BAD company." The voice was low, obviously filtered through a distortion device.

Stay silent, Oscar thought. *Or end them.*

"Mafia hands. Mafia company. Or did you not know that?"

Oscar recalled a holiday from three months ago. He had headed East and simply wanted daily fresh seafood with a bit of extravagance. He'd heard some of the higher-end hotels in Manila were nice so ventured there. Then came news of big scores at the gambling table. He had the money. He could afford the loss if it came to it. He could also afford the win if he got that, too. Every nickel and dime to grow his empire. But these games . . . they were no nickel-and-dimers. A nickel was five hundred grand. A dime was a million. Big risk . . . but potential big reward too. He just didn't know the gentlemen he was playing with were killers until one of them whispered news to another, something about cement shoes and a black bag with two hundred and fifty thousand in it. Two hundred and fifty-three and a half, if Oscar wanted to be specific.

Both sides of his eye sockets burst into a dull drone of pain. Something wasn't right. He could take a strike from Axiom-man and keep going. Whoever was doing this had the ability to strike on surprise and disappear, and strike precisely on the nerve centers all over his head.

"Stop it!" he spat.

"You are a rich man, Mr. Owen," the voice said.

A deep penetrating punch forced his stomach inward then it settled back out. How was this person hitting him so fast then quickly getting out of view.

"I know you're behind me," Oscar said. "What do you want? Money? Name a price. I'll pay, and this will be forgotten."

"Money from what?"

"I'm a businessman. I have mo—"

"You are not. You are scum. You accumulate wealth off the books through illegal means." The person went quiet. Good. Then, "Crime is crime, Mr. Owen. Your philanthropy means nothing nor does it make atonement."

Crime. Do they know I'm Redsaw?

"I don't know what you're talking about," he said.

"Philippines. Poker. Mafia."

"I was on holiday. So what?"

"Philippines. Poker. Mafia."

"I never played cards there. Just went sight-seeing and unwound with drinks and some company."

"Philippines. Poker. Mafia."

"Okay, the company was a few young women."

"Philippines. Poker. Mafia."

He kept his anger in check despite how badly Redsaw wanted out. It would be a fast kill if he acted. "They were of age, I swear. I checked. Do you think someone of my stature would want to be caught with a minor?"

"Philippines. Poker. Mafia."

"Stop saying that!"

"Philippines. Poker. Mafia."

"Stop it!" This time what felt like a heavy chunk of wood struck his forehead, knocking his head back and causing a pinch at the base of his neck.

"Philippines. Poker. Mafia."

"Quiet!"

"Philippines. Poker. Maf—" Another strike, this one under his chin, the soft part before the jawbone. He gagged, spat, then breathed slowly, carefully regaining air without choking.

They didn't finish their sent—A sharp sting lit up the rims of both ears then pain radiated into both ears. This person was trained.

"You don't want to do this," Oscar said. The words were intentionally pleading. Redsaw stirred inside, and Oscar got a mental picture of the beast as a red and black-striped tiger, bloodthirsty, angry, pacing the cage. Firmly, "You do not. Want. To. Do. This."

It went dark.

———

Valerie sat at home on the couch, head resting against the back cushion. Work was busy. Her brain was tired.

And Gabriel was on the news.

She raised her phone to her eyes and scrolled the headlines. They were all worded in different ways but the message was the same: Axiom-man has gone rogue. Again.

"Don't they remember that it was Redsaw masquerading as Axiom-man before? No. Of course not. That doesn't sell papers and get clicks."

Yet she couldn't help but wonder if that's who was out there bringing down all those buildings. Gabriel wouldn't do that. As powerful as he was, he understood restraint and self-control even under pressure.

"I hope it isn't you," she said. "But if it is? I know you well enough to know you have a reason." *A good one.* She took a deep breath. *It better be.*

She straightened, set her phone on the coffee table, then leaned forward, elbows on her knees. She wanted Gabriel to come home, to fill her in, to bring her alongside so she could support him or help him somehow.

She got up, crossed the room, passed by the bedroom and at quick glance, noticed Gabriel's side of the bed was relatively tidy, meaning he didn't come home to rest. Gabriel never made the bed after sleeping in it.

"Why bother?" he once said. "You're just gonna be back in it in around fourteen hours anyway."

Typical guy thinking, she had thought then. Now she wished she saw a layer of messy sheets.

She couldn't quite place it, but she had a feeling that after whatever was going on, her and Gabriel's relationship would never be the same.

Chapter Ten

WHEN OSCAR CAME to, his legs were rubbery as were his arms. But he was standing. How he could have been unconscious then put in a standing position for waking up, he didn't know, but he was standing and without binds. Across the room, through blurry vision, a figure stood, clad in gray head to toe, a hood and cloak draped over head and shoulders. The clothing, it was hard to tell through the fog, but it appeared almost militaristic, like a soldier's thick battle uniform before hitting the frontlines. He noticed some pockets and pouches but couldn't make out much else. Besides, a good portion of this person's body was covered by the cloak.

Play the card one last time. "What do you want?" he asked, sounding as exhausted and desperate as possible.

"Justice."

The figure approached, their footfalls utterly silent despite the boots moving along the cement floor. Either this person was floating a mere millimeter from the ground, or they had the ability to move with such stealth it was no wonder they got in as many strikes against Oscar as they had.

Oscar took a breath. "You shouldn't come any closer."

The figure stopped but seemingly not from the threat. Oscar got a better look at them, namely the face overshadowed by the hood. The stitch work showed one section was for the mouth, another for around the eyes, the other for the rest of the head. He peered into the figure's eyes, hoping to see eyeballs. Dark gray lenses covered the eyes.

The two remained silent for a solid three or four minutes before the figure began its approach again.

Oscar held out a hand. "Stay back." He glanced up at the cameras. They were off. At least, he couldn't see any flashing light indicating they were on. He still had to be careful.

The figure raised an arm, showing its hand and splaying out its fingers while still approaching.

"One more step, I'm warning you, and I'll—I'll have my lawyers and the police turn this place inside out with you as prime target."

The figure stopped, as if contemplating. "Do you fear the law, Mr. Owen?"

"I, um, yes, yes, of course I do. I'm a law-abiding citizen. I don't want any trouble."

"Philippines. Poker. Mafia."

"That's enough!" he shouted. The red-and-black tiger swatted at the cage's bars, its sharp claws scraping down the metal on the descent.

"It's never enough."

The figure moved forward, side-stepped, and in a blur of motion delivered a kick to Oscar's middle, striking where his gut met the bottom of his rib cage. He spit out a glob of vomit.

The tiger roared then lowered its rage into a haunting growl.

"You . . . don't . . ." He threw up again then spat out the rest. "Stop." The word was meant to be firm but came out feeble.

The tiger's eyes went bloodshot and it peeled back its lips, revealing sharp fangs, teeth destined to destroy and tear apart its prey.

"You are a criminal, Oscar."

You have no idea.

"Pay your account," the figure ordered.

At first Oscar's mind went to finances but then he quickly understood that's not what the figure was referring to. "You have the wrong guy."

The inside of a foot cracked across his cheekbone. He only saw the foot for a split second before the impact. How this person could raise their legs so fast and without telegraphing, he didn't know. The shock of the blow dropped him to his knees.

The tiger struck the cage; this time its claws peeled strands of metal from the bars.

Those cameras. They cannot be on. No one can know. No one can—A strike to his hamstrings and his legs buckled beneath him, his backside now resting on his heels. He knew he had the strength to stand despite the pain. He just wasn't sure if now was the ti—The figure was upon him and his shoulder blades caught fire, locked up, and forced him forward so he was completely folded over his thighs.

Prison. A self-contained prison of the body. This is no ordinary—The tiger's eyes narrowed.

Hands grabbed him by the collar, drew him upright then threw him back down so hard he was knocked flat on his shoulder blades, his legs still folded in a kneeling position. The sharp pain of over-stretched muscles blasted through his thighs and hip flexors. The pressure in his knees indicated their own strain.

The tiger swiped at the bars, dislodging another slice of metal.

The gray figure stood over him, the cloak down to its ankles, dirty around its hem.

"How much do you want?" Oscar asked.

"More than you can pay," the figure said and slammed its fist down like a hammer where his ribcage covered his heart. The wind left him and he gasped for air. His body jerked so hard it untangled him from his folded-back position and flipped him on his side.

The tiger took its final swipe.

Oscar breathed hard and fast then slammed the underside of his fist against the cement, cracking it in a jagged spider web.

The figure didn't seem fazed. Did it know?

"Last time," Oscar said, his voice dark and low. Redsaw's voice.

The figure put a boot on top of the fist that struck the ground as if trying to dig his hand further into the cement.

Red tiger.

His power filled his fist, its red energy and heat forcing the figure to remove its boot. The moment the boot left his hand, he swung his arm in an arc, red energy taking out the cameras in the corners of the room.

Oscar stood.

"Redsaw," the figure said.

"At your service."

———

Valerie headed home. Most likely Gabriel wouldn't be there. And if he was . . . he still wouldn't be there. Not in the truest sense. There was a big difference between being present in body and present in mind.

I don't know what's wrong with you and, to be honest, I'm scared. Not of you. Of course not, Gabriel. Never you. "It's just that I'm seeing a side," she whispered. "A side I don't understand."

She was more aware of the world she lived in. Super feats, unusual people, outfits that stood out—all that was the norm.

And all that was in the media.

She was getting a glimpse of the *inside,* the real inside of all this. This wasn't simply about good versus evil, though that's what it could be distilled to, but that was an oversimplification. The core truth was there were so many peripherals the public wasn't aware of.

Like the peripheral of the battle destroying a man.

Like the peripheral of the battle slowly degenerating a relationship.

That one hurt. As much as Valerie tried to sympathize and empathize with Gabriel, she knew she would never truly connect with him on those levels. She couldn't. It was impossible. She wasn't him, and only he knew every jot and tittle of what he was going through. He could explain and vent and talk it out, but that would never fully set her on the same page. Partially on the page, sure, but never fully on it.

Gabriel was his own book.

One that was being burned.

———

The figure in gray dove to the side when a blast of red energy headed straight toward it. Quickly, the figure rolled along the ground toward Oscar—or was he Redsaw now despite not wearing the red and black outfit?—and delivered a swift blow to Oscar's gut. Oscar teetered backward and bent slightly forward from the blow. With a growl, he lashed out, red streams of energy pouring from his fingers.

The figure avoided the blast, which took out the wall to their left, the same wall that, now he noticed, oversaw the street below.

Oscar rose into the air. "Gray hood. Gray cape. Gray outfit. Make it black!" He shot out more energy from his fists. The figure's hands moved so fast, they blurred with motion, then it rolled to the side, catching a portion of the blast in the cape, which erupted with flames. The figure rolled over the cape to put it out.

Oscar peered down at his own chest. It was dotted with three quarter-sized black circles about as thick as a checker piece. No sooner did he observe them did they burst, spraying up and around him thick plumes of dark gray smoke that reeked of sulfur. Eyes watering, coughing, barely able to draw clean air, Oscar flew out of the smoke, searched the room for his prey, found the figure, then flew straight toward it, knocking it to the ground. He pinned both their arms by the wrists above its head.

"You're about to lose your hands," Oscar said, a red glow growing around his fingers and fist.

"Good thing I'm insulated," said the voice.

A violent surge of harsh vibrating and painful electricity shot through Oscar's hands and up his arms, locking the muscles and making his shoulders pound. The voltage caused his neck to lock up and he couldn't turn or move his head in any direction.

A boot found its way between the figure and his chest.

The electricity abruptly stopped and the boot shot out, full leg extension, kicking him off.

Oscar stumbled backward and it seemed all his private Karate lessons had gone out the window. He was fairly adept at the training he took after work hours: old school

Japanese Karate. Efficient. Quick. Harsh. And it worked. Whoever this was had studied something else. Something primal. Something basic. Something that enabled the fighter to cut to the heart of the conflict, find the opening, and take advantage of it before the other person could react.

No sooner was he on his feet did the rough sole of the boot strike him square in the nose. Another blow hit his throat and something hard smashed into both his kneecaps, forcing the joint against itself, straining it, causing his legs to buckle and fall out from beneath him.

I will not bend my knee to a mere mortal with some tricks! He tried to stand but the ligaments and tendons surrounding the joints were strained and it was difficult to find the strength to get up. He tapped into all he had and got to his feet, taking shallow breaths as he rose until things calmed down and he could breathe freely again.

"Very good," Oscar said.

The gray figure merely stared at him, its eyes concealed behind some sort of lens he couldn't discern, at least not at this the distance.

The two stood facing each other, unmoving, silent.

The seconds ticked by.

Oscar eyed the figure up and down. Its stance and posture made the body language impossible to read. It just stood there, hands at its sides, feet casually together.

As if waiting for something.

The seconds turned to a minute.

Neither moved.

It's trying to get in my head, Oscar thought. *Intimidation through inaction.* His heart rate picked up in anticipation of the next strike. *Treat this guy like Axiom-man. Don't hold back. End them.*

THE SUMMONING

As fast as he could, Oscar clenched his fists, reached his arms forward, and flew head on at the figure. The figure raised its arms high, as if in welcome, and let Oscar grab it around the waist and fly it out through the wall.

Oscar took the figure in gray another hundred feet in the air, swiftly reversed course, then flew as fast as he could straight toward the ground.

The figure did not struggle in his arms. With a slight movement of its hand a loud hissing sound broke out, like a high-pressure air leak.

A loud pop sounded behind him and Oscar looked out of instinct. Something red had dispersed high in the air.

The sound clicked in his brain.

A flare gun.

About to hit the street, what felt like a battering ram plowed into him, grabbed them both, then swooped around and lowered them to street level.

Axiom-man.

He can't know. Does he? Did he see anything? "Oh, thank goodness. This person—" He pointed to the figure in gray. "Somehow got me in the air and I didn't know what to do and . . ."

The figure in gray kicked him in the chin. "Quiet," it said.

Axiom-man put a hand on the figure in gray's shoulder. Oscar could tell by the way the gray fabric bunched up beneath those blue fingers he tightly gripped the person.

"Sir—" Axiom-man started but quickly stopped. He turned to the side. His body lurched in a bizarre wiggle of forced self-containment. "Sir." The words were barely audible.

The gray figure moved in toward Oscar and delivered a hooking punch to the side his head. Though Oscar could have taken the blow, he played into it and dropped to the ground, holding the side of his head. "Ow. Ouch. Oww."

Next thing Oscar knew, both arms had him and his feet left the ground as Axiom-man flew to the nearest street a couple blocks away.

"Run," Axiom-man said.

The way the man in blue looked at him. Something wasn't right. Oscar supposed it was possible one day Axiom-man would learn his true identity. He just didn't expect it'd be today.

Oscar ran. When he glanced back over his shoulder, Axiom-man was gone.

CHAPTER ELEVEN

AXIOM-MAN'S BLUE CAPE was up and over his head and wrapped around his face the second he landed in front of the figure in gray. He started untangling it but that'd take too long so he fired up his eye beams and blasted clean through it, the hole big enough to see through and enough to loosen the cape's bind around his head. A flying ridged sole of a boot came straight for his face. Before he could use his eye beams to shoot it out of the way, it struck him square on and knocked his neck back hard. When he righted his head, a profound pain shot through his ankle and it folded underneath him. Down on one knee, he shot a warning blast of energy into the brick wall beyond the gray figure, hoping it'd be enough to deter it. Instead, the figure merely peered back at the damage then back at him.

"You're not ready," the figure said.

"What are you talking about?" Axiom-man asked.

The hooded figure didn't answer.

Axiom-man got to his feet, careful not to set too much weight upon his ankle. He flew straight at the figure, grabbed the person around the waist, and flew them into the wall next to the damage he wrought. The figure grunted on impact. Axiom-man had controlled the force enough to rattle them but not hard enough to kill them or break their bones.

A sharp yet dull pain stabbed into the left side of his neck. A knife? He didn't feel the moisture of blood and the person's hands were empty of any weapon.

His throat seized up.

The figure in gray simply held up two ridged fingers then used them to point to its neck. Whatever it had done, it had pin-pointed a nerve center, causing everything to tighten and lock up.

"How does it feel to not breathe?" the figure asked. "Of course, no doubt, you've been in this position before—unable to breathe. But are the circumstances different? A mere touch and, if I wanted, I could control you. Consider this a warning."

Axiom-man gagged and rubbed at the aching spot. When he glanced up, the gray figure was gone.

He coughed, gasped, coughed again. Slowly, air returned. Who was that caped person in gray and what did they want with Oscar Owen?

Immediately, Axiom-man's mind went to Oscar. The man . . . he couldn't quite place it. Something wasn't right with that man. Being around him had caused Axiom-man's insides to swim and to feel a little weak.

He knew that feeling.

Redsaw.

The presence of the man, the darkness within, the other side of the balance—he was evil. His very aura stuck to things, contaminated the environment.

What was Valerie's boss doing around Redsaw?

———

I should have taken him, Oscar thought. *He was right there. He even had me in his arms. I could have ended him quietly, away from any onlookers. If he figured out who I was, it wouldn't matter at that point. He'd be dead.* That figure in gray. Whoever it was, it was an interference and an extremely talented fighter. Oscar did not notice any meta abilities except, perhaps, for enhanced speed. It was the only explanation he could give to the fact its strikes seemed to come out of nowhere and without warning, telegraphing—anything.

"Or they're just *really* good," he said quietly.

He couldn't go back to work. Not now. Not after that.

There was only one place he could go: The sky.

———

Axiom-man landed in front of a looter hauling a TV out of a pawn shop window. The device was too big and wide and its awkwardness caused the man to drop it.

Axiom-man tapped him on the shoulder. "Ahem."

The man turned and was greeted with a punch to the face that dropped him.

An explosion rang out down the street, perhaps a couple sidewalk lengths away. Axiom-man took off toward it, eyes wide, his peripheral vision purposefully taking in everything around him. He had to keep an eye out for Redsaw. He probably wasn't around here but it never hurt to be alert.

A wall of flame suddenly flared up in front of him.

"Hahaha," came a female voice. It took a moment but Axiom-man recognized it: Lady Fire.

The woman was in the air, fluttering her ladybug-like wings, circling him, fire and brimstone flowing from her hands, lighting up and igniting anything combustible around him. Axiom-man rose into the air above the flame and headed straight for her.

He knew this fight.

He knew *her*. She might have been a sweet lady at one point, but obviously something happened that changed all that. Or, she might have been a psycho to begin with and obtaining powers—if she wasn't born with them—only drove her over the edge. Axiom-man didn't understand why, out of all those with special abilities he'd encountered, all of them had used their power for evil. Was it by design? Those powers? Even his? Did the powers in and of themselves have some sort of moral code? Good powers and bad powers? The kind that changed you into whatever it wanted you to be?

For a moment, Axiom-man considered he'd been brainwashed, that his powers from the messenger also influenced his behavior. No, couldn't be. He remembered his choice as to how to use them. He remembered reading about that little girl in the paper and that being the catalyst to donning the mask. Or did his powers influence his reaction to her tale? Did they make him make the choice on how to use them? He knew full well the messenger had full control over his abilities. The messenger had the power to manipulate them if needed. Allow *surges* and being told why those *surges* occur, which was all based on power usage and the reasons for their use.

Stewardship.

A gust of flame to his left jolted Axiom-man from his thoughts and ignited his cape, causing him to twist mid-air and head toward the ground outside of Lady Fire's range. Axiom-man hit the pavement, rolled over his cape and put the flames out.

I am *tired,* he thought. *Lost my head while in a fight. Come on. Focus.* It wasn't so much a thought as it was a feeling but he sensed Lady Fire coming right at him. The second her body made impact, he wrapped his arms around her and took her as high as possible until the air was so cold every breath was sharp ice in his lungs.

"I don't have time for this," he told her softly but with a grunt.

Lady Fire coughed. "What . . . what're yo—" She coughed again, the icy, thin air clearly making it hard for her to speak.

Her body went limp then ridged then limp then ridged as she fought against passing out.

To keep from passing out himself, Axiom-man only took in air when he needed to, holding what oxygen he could in his lungs until fully absorbed before attempting another breath. If he gauged his breathing, he could outlast her and . . .

Tremendous heat seared into the side of his face. Had she put her hand directly on him or—All he saw was her hand drop by her side. Face burning, unsure if his mask was even still intact, Axiom-man secured his grip on Lady Fire and dove down toward the earth with her in his arms. The rush of wind would put out any fire on his face if there was some or, at least, cool the fabric of his mask and possibly skin enough to help deal with the hot pain.

When he touched down, Lady Fire was dead weight in his arms. He laid her on the ground then touched his face. The side of his mask was burned away and his skin was fiercely sensitive. Possibly second-degree burns. He could only imagine what he might look like without his mask on. The thought of her disfiguring him made him temporarily want to kick her while she lay unconscious . . . but there was no point. He needed a mirror and now was not the time for vanity.

Frustrated, he grabbed Lady Fire by her black collar and dragged her body along the ground to the nearest dumpster. He picked her up and dropped her in, bringing down the partially open lid all the way closed. Energy filling his eyes, he rounded to the back end of the dumpster, picked the corner near the hinge, then let the energy flow out as he walked around the dumpster in a semi-circle, sealing the lid to the metal of the bin. At least she'll be contained and she'd be all right air-wise for a while despite the awful and thick stench of trash. Most likely she'd burn her way out, but if Gunn could pick her up before then, then she'd be put away and be one less thing for Axiom-man to worry about.

Axiom-man got on the comm with Gunn. "Lady Fire. First dumpster at Bannatyne and Main. Sealed. You can't miss it."

"How dare you—" Gunn started but was cut off when Axiom-man turned off the comm. This wasn't a time to bicker with Gunn, and he was done being told what to do. Gunn's original assignment to cover the air and search for Redsaw hadn't worked out. It was too basic of a plan, and while true that the simplest plan is usually the most efficient one, there were exceptions and Redsaw certainly was one. Things were never simple with Redsaw. Not that the man in black and red created chaotic and convoluted plans. No, Redsaw had demonstrated time and time again there were brains beneath that black cowl. Redsaw's complexity was because he was smart. He didn't always show it, but due to Axiom-man's connection with him through their powers, he sensed every action Redsaw committed was deliberate despite how it might look from the outside. Even a simple fist fight was more than that regardless of how it was perceived. Redsaw took hits on purpose, Axiom-man figured, took defeat, took being out-witted—because it was all part of a larger plan.

Axiom-man knew from his own experience wearing the cape a larger plan was critical for someone with his powers. For *anyone* with powers. Having powers forced you to look at the big picture, to consider the butterfly effect of the power's use, to look not just past the moment but into the future to how ultra-powered action could have long-term ramifications. Perhaps it was taking the short view that led to these people's downfall, the misuse of the power they've been given.

"Stop it," Axiom-man told himself.

He needed to sleep. His mind was going every which way and philosophizing over things when practical thought and steps needed to be taken.

A wave of fatigue struck him and he swooned on his feet.

He was going down.

And time was running out.

CHAPTER TWELVE

REDSAW STOOD ATOP Owen Tower and overlooked the city. Chaos still rang below but seemed to be simmering down. A good loot and riot could only go on for so long before people ran out of energy. It didn't matter at this point. Redsaw had made his statement.

This city was his.

Soon, so would the province, then the country, then more. But he also knew his master would only let him have so much. At least, where things stood at the moment. But if Axiom-man was to die, maybe then his master would let him have more. More power. More control. More territory.

Simply . . . more.

Redsaw eyed the metal tower atop his own monument to self. These were installed on top of every property he owned, and even on some others he didn't. Just give the owner the right amount of money and well, you could do what you wanted. Everyone, Redsaw knew, had a price tag. Every soul on the planet. The only thing separating people from each other in that regard was simply everybody's number was different and one could assume or ballpark that number just by getting to know someone. That method led to many business deals in his favor. It also led to more savings than expected because some staunch capitalists just took what they could get dollar-wise, amount be damned. Money was money and the more the better.

Foolish humans, Redsaw thought. Then he caught himself. Humans. He had called them humans.

His mind went blank at the notion. Then the acknowledgement he had separated himself from them crept in, and he wasn't sure what to think or feel. The confusion made his heart sink.

No, he thought. "I'm human too. Was human. Am human. Started human. Am I human?"

The only conclusion he could draw before he noticed a flicker of light blue fly past him over a street below was he wasn't human. At least in the purest sense. He could do things other humans couldn't. That made him different . . .

. . . and so it also made the man who just flew by his building different.

———

All Axiom-man wanted to do was go home and see Valerie. Then he remembered she was at work and he'd come home to an empty apartment. Maybe it was better that way, especially since his face might be burned halfway to hell.

Axiom-man landed on the balcony and entered as quickly as possible so as not to be seen. The moment he was inside, he carefully and slowly pulled down his mask, the brush of the fabric against his burnt skin sending a shockwave of sharp tingles through his face and head and down the side of his neck. He *shifted* and powered down. He was Gabriel again.

He needed a mirror and a lot of Advil. As he walked toward the bathroom mirror, the mild breeze of air brushing his sensitive and exposed skin made each step forward painful.

Just take it and see the damage. He entered the bathroom, lights off. He stood in front of the mirror. As much as he wanted to see his face, he didn't want to see his face.

Man, he was tired. His eyes ached from fatigue and collapsing into bed seemed like an extremely good idea.

But his face.

Eyes closed, he flicked on the light. He silently counted to three. *Just look. Don't react. Just look first. Keep it simple.* He opened his eyes. From his left cheekbone, down his cheek and along his jawline, was deep red skin with light blisters slightly raised on top.

Gabriel stared at himself for a long time. This wasn't the man he knew. This wasn't the person he was even a short time ago.

This was a warrior.

And though the notion uplifted his spirits some, it wasn't enough to compensate for the ugly visage before him. He leaned closer to the mirror and touched gloved fingers to his skin. Even the material upon his fingertips caused the wound to sting, but from what he could tell, he had received second-degree burns at worst, maybe terrible first-degree burns at best. He needed a doctor. He also knew from past experience he'd need an excuse for the injury and a doctor that would keep his or her mouth shut should they discover his special abilities as they examined him or took bloodwork or ran any other tests.

He went to the bedroom, took his uniform off, put on a T-shirt and sweats, then hit the bathroom again. From the cabinet, he took out the Advil and a small jar of Vaseline. He downed a half dozen pills then carefully and gently applied the Vaseline to the burn. At least this way there'd be a barrier between the burn and the air thus protecting it from possible contamination and infection.

He looked like a slime monster. It was indeed good Valerie wasn't here. She probably wouldn't recognize him unless he spoke.

Gabriel went to the kitchen, opened the freezer, and took out an ice pack. He pressed it to his face. Though he knew the effort wouldn't do much as the cold should have been applied the instant he got burned, he figured even a small effort was better than no effort. Helped ease the pain, though.

He took the ice pack to the bedroom and fell back on the bed, head hitting the pillow. He lay there, staring at the ceiling, ice pack against his cheek, the sick feeling of utter failure penetrating his heart and sinking it into his stomach.

"I can't do this," he whispered. "I'm not strong enough." *I'm human despite the powers.* Despite all he could do, he still ran on ordinary calories and sleep like everybody else. Sure, when shifted into Axiom-man mode he had a plethora of energy, but even that had limits and right now, that was tapped out. Whatever damage Redsaw had intended for the city was now done. The ball was too big and was in full rolling force. The best Gabriel could do was get as many people out of its path as possible.

"I just . . ." he said. "I just can't find him."

———

Redsaw had kept his distance while trailing Axiom-man. He hadn't wanted to alert the man in blue to his presence. But Redsaw did see where he landed. Did see him go inside an apartment balcony's door.

He just needed to know who lived at the address.

———

It stood a ways back from the building's ledge so as not to be seen. It was an old trick and one that was quite obvious, but the figure in gray never understood why Axiom-man insisted on always appearing standing proud on the building's ledge.

Maybe just to let people know he's out there, the figure thought. Its thick cape billowed about it, the wind picking up. Its uniform was dense, thick material intended for motorcyclists never mind the padding underneath. But it was all dark gray, head to toe, the hood overshadowing its face, darkening the mask it wore. But this old trick, the one of staying away from sight, it was the same trick the Crimson Cloak used back in the '20s. The figure was confident nobody in the city of Winnipeg knew that person ever existed. There were no headlines. Any pummelled troublemakers never said a word. The beat cops at the time were silent. That was, if they knew. There was nothing in Winnipeg's written history that indicated a red vigilante from roughly a hundred years ago existed. But the figure knew about him. Knew what he did. It had to know. It was a matter of, simply, backwards engineering. Winnipeg's criminal structure—especially organized crime—had its roots somewhere. It was a common misconception that cutting off the head of the snake, the leaders of the crime families, would bring peace. That never worked because the snake always grew a new head. Sometimes it took time, but eventually it emerged and usually emerged with a vengeance. Cut off the top of a tree, it'll find a way to sprout and keep going atop its peak.

There was only one way to cut down a tree: as close to the roots as possible and, if you were really thorough, you'd take out the roots themselves and ensure they'd

THE SUMMONING

Valerie watched Gabriel stand by the balcony window, coffee in hand, slowly sipping as he looked out onto the city.

Something's for sure not right with him. I've never seen him so devoted to Axiom-man like this. He takes the mantle seriously, and I've always known that, but this is something else. This transcends mere duty to use his powers for good things. There's something he's not telling me. Or I'm being paranoid. Gabriel's always been up front with me. Maybe I'm *the one who needs to understand.* "Or maybe I understand plenty," she said.

"Hm?" Gabriel turned in her direction.

"What? Nothing. Just thinking out loud."

He turned back to the window.

"What are you going to do?" she asked already knowing the answer.

He faced her and lowered the arm with the coffee. "I don't know. I mean, I *know* what I have to do. It's more so the how. I'm . . . I'm sorry, Valerie. Truly. This is new to you, I know. Despite all I've told you—which is everything I know about how all this works—it's not something you can just speak to and say, 'Okay, thanks for telling me. I can move ahead now.' If I'm confused, I can only imagine how you must be feeling."

"Not good," she said softly.

"I know." He put a hand to her cheek but removed it quicker than she would've liked. "If we" —he looked out the window again— "if we go slow, at least, as slow as allowed given the circumstances and think things through, we'll come out okay. I'm talking both the city and us."

"But which is more important?" It was a selfish question, she knew, but it came out before she could keep it inside.

Gabriel glanced down. She wasn't sure if she saw disappointment in his eyes or just fatigue, but she knew he didn't like the question any more than she did.

He raised his head. "Both."

———

The figure in gray entered the dank warehouse, long unused that reminded them of an event of their past. The place was mostly barren with a few boxes and rickety crates here and there. The room was covered in shadow everywhere; the light from windows running horizontally high along the side of the building didn't shed much illumination.

"I can hear you," the figure in gray said.

"No, you can't." The woman stepped out of the darkness. "How did you really know I was there? Give me the right answer."

"Deductive reasoning."

"That's better."

And the woman was right. That was the correct answer. The woman was a person of silence. Her footsteps inaudible. Her breathing hidden. Her ability to rise and recede from the darkness a mystery. This woman wasn't . . . normal.

"Clouds are coming," the woman said. "Both physical and to the lives of the people. We are about to descend into the pit and there is no going around it."

"So the time has come?"

"Not so much time. That's putting it too simply. More so the cosmos begs for balance and going down into the pit is the only way to get it."

CHAPTER FOURTEEN

AXIOM-MAN TAPPED ON the glass of the window to Jack Gunn's office. The curtain was down, probably for security and not just privacy. Security so no one could see who or what was inside.

The curtain drew back and Gunn's face filled the glass. He looked like hell, with his hair dishevelled and several days' worth of stubble all over his cheeks and neck. Axiom-man could only guess at the last time the man changed his clothes because the vintage brown-striped button-down held what looked like coffee stains patched over his chest.

There was a series of clicks then the window was drawn open.

"Locked," Axiom-man said.

"Safety," Gunn replied. His tone was flat and he immediately turned his back on Axiom-man as he entered the room.

Gunn stood a few meters from him, hands on hips, back still turned.

Axiom-man stood there, allowing his cape to conceal most of his body as if a kind of shield against what he knew would be Gunn's wrath. He was also grateful for his back-up mask. At least it would conceal his true face and the damage thereon.

Both men stood in silence. Axiom-man knew it'd probably be best if Gunn had the first word.

The silence went on.

Axiom-man breathed steadily through his nose, keeping any possible anxiousness at bay. Not that he feared Gunn. He just didn't like hearing the man yell.

"I'm not going to yell," Gunn said, back still turned. Though he was speaking to Axiom-man, his words seemed directed at the wall across from him. "But I want to," he said firmly. "You have no concept of the beast within right now."

"I'm sorry."

"Sorry's not good enough," Gunn said. "None of it is anymore."

Axiom-man waited.

"You had an assignment," Gunn said, "and yeah, yeah, you don't work for the police so I can't officially give you orders but at the same time, I'm an officer of the law which obligates you to listen at the minimum." Gunn sighed, turned around and faced him, took a look, then turned away again. "Maybe this is my fault. I gave you orders and you followed them . . . but then reneged. Maybe I didn't see the defiance as inevitable."

"I wasn't defying you, Jack."

"Don't use my first name. We're not friends."

"No, but allies."

Gunn took a slow breath then exhaled. "Not that anymore either."

A small jolt of surprise shot through Axiom-man's heart. He knew the Winnipeg Police Service hated him, but Gunn? *Maybe "hate" is too strong a word,* he thought.

"You went rogue on an entire city, boy in blue. You took down buildings. What's worse, you might have thought it was safe to do so, but do you know what? It wasn't. There were people near each fall and each one of them got injured. Thankfully, no one died so good for you. You get props there, but your job isn't to hurt people."

"No."

"But you did. And you were reckless, uncaring, and, boy, you don't need to say it, but acted like a desperate man."

"I am desperate."

Gunn flung around to face him. "And at what cost? Dollars? Millions. People? Priceless. And you don't seem to know the difference."

Gunn had it all wrong, Axiom-man knew, but he was also aware the man needed to get it out of his system. "Remember when the city thought I went full enemy and it turned out to be him?

Gunn didn't reply.

"Did that not show that not all is what it seems?"

"You have zero intellect if you think that's a viable comparison. It's one thing for a nutjob to put on a costume and cause trouble under the guise of this city's . . . saviour; quite another when it's the saviour himself." Sweat ran down Gunn's cheeks, and though the lighting wasn't all that great in here, his face clearly turned red. "What's the matter with you?" he shouted.

There it was. Finally. Axiom-man knew Gunn couldn't keep it in for long. He kept as calm and non-reactive as he could. "There was no other option."

"There is always another option!"

"Then tell me how to find this man, straight to him. A to B. Do you have that?" It was sarcasm but it was the only way to make the point. "The man has unleashed everyone dangerous that I've stopped. They're still out there, undefeated, and he's . . . Redsaw's . . . out there, undefeated as well."

"You're in over your head." Gunn swung out an arm with a finger pointing toward the window. "Surely, you might have slowed things down a bit out there but slowing down a speeding train by a few klicks an hour doesn't make a dent. You have failed." Gunn's eyes slightly widened when he said that and though the man might not have meant to say it, he was being honest.

Axiom-man bowed his head then raised it. "Yeah, I have failed. It's me versus everyone."

"It is. Including versus me." Gunn reached behind his back then dangled a pair of handcuffs in front of him. "Axiom-man, you are under arrest for reckless endangerment, aiding and abetting multiple criminals, and the use of brute force with intent."

"I am not helping them."

"Yes, you are. When you don't stop them, you assist their need to exert force on others, often resulting in death."

"That's not abetting."

"It is now. You're driving their anger, their plans, their execution of those plans. They're not after just anybody. You know that. They're after *you*."

Axiom-man kept his hands at his side.

Gunn held out the cuffs farther in front of him. "Please come with me quietly."

Axiom-man drew his hands out from behind his cape, looked at them, then drew them back. "Then I'm sorry, my friend. We are at war."

Gunn pulled his weapon. Axiom-man shot it out of his hand with his eye beams, floated into the air, then darted out the window right after Gunn picked up the firearm off the floor and aimed it again.

———

Axiom-man headed straight skyward, spiking through the clouds like a nail through a hand.

Grimacing, he poured on as much speed as he could. He didn't care how high he flew, how cold it got, how thin the air would turn—he just needed away from this stupid planet for a moment's peace.

Too bad I can't just leave, he thought as he rocketed upward. He knew he'd have to turn back. He wasn't invincible and could not live without air. Eventually, he'd have to swallow his pride and turn around and at least go low enough so there was, comparatively, little distance between him and the ground.

But right now? He had to keep going up.

———

"The problem with the Internet is everybody is online," Oscar said as he punched the address of the building he saw Axiom-man enter into the search engine. What came up was what he already knew: the name and location of the apartment building. He hit streetview and did a virtual reconnaissance as much as the imaging would allow. It was an older view. He knew this solely because of the change in color of the flowers out front. But there were no leads or way to find out who lived in what sui— there! Sometimes a simple question got a simple answer. Contact information for the landlord and better, the name of the property firm that owned the building.

For a brief moment, the idea of simply buying the building to find out its tenants crossed his mind, but outside of a potential headache dealing with landlords who may or may not be trustworthy, Oscar figured again.

And again.

And again.

He would make the call.

———

Axiom-man stopped his flight straight up and shouted into the sky, "Why couldn't have you made me stronger!" It was meant for the messenger. Then he realized what he said and how unfair it was. The messenger had given him great power and, throughout the course of using them for the right purpose, occasionally granted a *surge* in a particular ability. Axiom-man didn't like the *surges*; he did like the aftereffects. But during a *surge* when a power went haywire, there was little control and the strength or the speed—it was difficult for his mind to keep up. Only when things powered down and settled to their new level was he finally at ease.

He could only hope his comment didn't provoke the messenger into withdrawing some or all of his power. He couldn't afford that. Not today. Not even tomorrow.

Not until Redsaw was dead.

———

The figure in gray had been on top of the old Bank of Montreal building when Axiom-man had flown out of the window of City Hall and headed straight into the sky.

"You need to focus," it said. "You're playing right into his hand. Come down. Calm down."

The figure turned then ran at the building's ledge and dove off, cape billowing out around it. A quick line of a slow-descent grapple shot out from the shadows within the cape.

"I'll help you soon enough."

———

Valerie stood staring at the empty bed. She stepped out of the room then stared at the empty couch. For a quick second, she saw her and Gabriel cuddled up together on that couch watching a movie, popcorn between them, some kernels in Gabriel's lap because he always spilled his snacks.

And not as an act either as some sort of clumsy identity.

If anything, Valerie wasn't sure where Gabriel stood on the whole dual-identity thing. He had told her he'd made a mistake creating a slightly over-the-top-ordinary-citizen persona to mask him being Axiom-man. The disguise certainly worked. Fooled her. Gabriel wore two masks: the glasses, and the Axiom-man one. She wasn't sure if she should feel warmth at his effort of identity concealment to protect himself and others, or if she should be furious at him for never really being himself.

That wasn't true.

She took it back.

He *was* himself with her. He wasn't Gabriel the nerd. He wasn't Axiom-man. He was just . . . Gabriel. But then, she realized, Gabriel didn't exist. Not anymore. She knew him once, a long time ago, back at Dolla-card before Axiom-man revealed himself to the city. Gabriel was just your regular guy so far as she knew. He was neither attractive nor unattractive. Just a average-looking guy who probably liked his sports and poker and a beer or three on the weekends. Stubble. The job being just that: a job.

She had to hand it to him, though. The change had been gradual. He played it smart and did it in such a way that—and also thanks to shift work—people hardly noticed it. It started with the stubble disappearing. At least, that's what Gabriel told her when they first talked about it. Just a smooth face, nothing more. Just something a man would naturally do if he wanted to keep it clean for a season. After that, the wardrobe slowly altered, going from business casual to dork. The colored shirts became slightly more awkward looking. Gabriel had said he had gone a size or two too big depending on the brand; plus, he said, the larger shirt helped conceal his uniform better. And he began taking better care of his hair. Well, "better" was something she'd say to loosely describe it. It had gone from a clean-cut style to getting a little long for parting to the side. Gabriel had mentioned the length was partly due to being lazy but also because the length helped cover part of his forehead thus concealing his face further once the glasses started being worn.

"You had it all planned out," she said quietly. "Did you plan for this?"

The empty apartment responded in silence, not of sound but of presence. This place was hollow without Gabriel home.

She circled back to wondering if it'd be a good idea for them to be around each other or not. She winced when a sharp pinch hit her heart. It's just that . . . it was true. All of it. Gabriel didn't exist. What she had on her hands was a mess of a man with combined identities all sewed and patched together into one.

She took in a slow, deep breath then exhaled just as smoothly. *You can't overreact. You've learned your lesson time and again that acting on emotion is a bad idea. You owe Gabriel your life several times over, and whether that was Gabriel doing it or Axiom-man, it doesn't matter. He helped you so now it's your turn to help him.*

How she could help him, she did not know.

CHAPTER FIFTEEN

GABRIEL WALKED PAST the computer in the apartment. Part of his deal with staying with Valerie was not just because they were a couple, but to do regular job hunting so she didn't have to carry the financial burden on her own.

He hadn't been looking for a job. Not when she wasn't home, and even if she was, he'd feign doing so. Instead, he was searching for clues as to Redsaw's whereabouts, any piece of new information that might help him track the man down.

It was a computer that started all this. It was the messenger's portal onto the Earth.

It was the night Gabriel got his powers.

Anger swelled within him and he briefly envisioned himself picking up that computer and throwing it across the room where it'd hit the wall and break into pieces. But what would that solve? Nothing. Just some misplaced but needed catharsis.

Gabriel sighed. "I need a way to pinpoint his location." He looked skyward. "I don't know if you can hear me but please don't take away my powers. Not yet. If that's what ends up happening at the end of all this, so be it but not yet. Please help me stop him." Gabriel didn't know if the messenger heard him or not, but right now, he hoped at minimum Someone was listening.

"Here you go, Mr. Owen," Valerie said as the man strode into reception area of his office. She handed him a stack of mail.

"Sorted?" he said.

"As requested and" —she lowered her voice— "as usual."

He didn't respond to the comment.

Oscar went into his office and closed the door behind him. He tossed the mail on the corner of his desk, sat down, set both elbows on the wooden top and put his chin on his hands. This . . . this seemed too easy. Either that or his master had orchestrated things to work out smoothly.

She was right outside his door.

All it took was one phone call between a developer and a property firm. A few discreet questions to test the waters. A wave of money—without intent of use, but they didn't need to know that—and a few charming words and Oscar got the firm to breach privacy and disclose the names of their tenants. At first, Oscar thought he had gotten it all wrong when he got the list. Every male tenant he looked at didn't quite fit the bill. Some were too old, so those were immediately ruled out. The others, some with occupations listed on the lease agreements, he couldn't see how those guys could manage their work and flying around. It wasn't until he came across a familiar name did he pause—Valerie's. It took him a moment to recall her last name. But he remembered: Vaughan. He looked into it a little further to confirm it wasn't just someone with the same name. A quick call to HR gave him the info he needed, and now he knew who Axiom-man had been spending his time with. In what capacity, he didn't know. And while deep down he didn't care, it was a piece of information that was important. He needed to know if Axiom-man just dropped in on her now and then and they had some sort of fling going on, or if there was something more to it. He checked to see if Valerie was registered with a roommate but she wasn't. It was just her name on the agreement.

Oscar had to somehow figure out who the man was that visited her.

———

Night.

The fires had died down thanks to a strong effort from Winnipeg's Fire Service. At most, there was a faint orange glow in the distance but that was about it. The air stank, a mix of smoke and garbage. Axiom-man could only imagine how much food, even people, were somewhere out there rotting, the scent rising on the air and mixing in with the ruin the city had become.

Black smoke quickly surrounded him. He didn't need to look around to know who it was: Bleaken.

"Like the Bible says," Bleaken said from somewhere in the dark, "I've been given permission to sift you as wheat except . . . no one has prayed for you that your faith may not fail!"

A hard strike from out of the darkness to Axiom-man's jaw made his head careen down and to the left. When he straightened, the same blow came in again. He lashed out, wildly swinging his fist into the dark and hitting nothing but smoke.

"You want to face me, Bleaken, come out of the shadows," Axiom-man said. He ensured his feet were planted good and firm on the rooftop.

Bleaken emerged from the dark, his body covered head to toe in swirling black cloud. It was hard to make out much else of him.

Axiom-man unleashed a blast of his eye beams, striking Bleaken and throwing him backward through the smoke to the other side of the cloud. Axiom-man walked through the dark and headed straight toward him.

"Who let you out?" Axiom-man said.

"Who do you think?" Bleaken shot out his hands, letting flow a thick elongated cloud of black smoke in Axiom-man's direction.

"Where is he?" Axiom-man remained in his spot. Firm. The glow running off his eyes kept things illuminated enough so he could see in the dark.

The blackness grew thicker.

"Bleaken, he's killing everybody. Tell me where he is!"

Silence.

With a growl, Axiom-man let blue power fill his eyes to the brim then let loose, spinning in a circle and cutting through the smoke, hoping he'd hit his adversary.

There was no sound of reaction.

Axiom-man powered down a little and took a good look at his surroundings.

Bleaken sprang at him out of the shadows and tackled him to the ground. Bleaken delivered several head and chest shots before Bleaken went for the ground-and-pound. Head spinning from the blows, Axiom-man managed to grab him by the wrists and slowly steer them away from his head and torso. He shot a knee into Bleaken's back and the dark man winced. He did it again and again, high and in between the shoulder blades.

Bleaken finally rolled off. Axiom-man hung on, getting rolled over on top of him. Axiom-man struck him in the face. "Location!"

Bleaken's voice deepened. "Sky."

Axiom-man hit him again. "Tell me!"

"Sky."

Both blue-gloved fists came down this time, the bottoms of his palms plowing into Bleaken's chest in an effort to wind him. It seemed to have worked because Bleaken started coughing.

Axiom-man gave him a hard slap with his palm against the cheekbone. "Where is Redsaw?"

"Sky."

Fire engulfed Axiom-man and Bleaken in an inferno. Axiom-man shoved his hands under Bleaken's underarms and hoisted the smoky figure upward, ascending over the smoke and flame, his cape ablaze. There was a faint feminine cackle somewhere nearby.

He moved and dropped Bleaken back down on the rooftop from twenty feet up while he beat the fire out of his cape. When he looked back down, Bleaken lay on the roof, one leg bent at the knee and folded beneath him. Axiom-man touched down, grabbed the man by the cloth of his suit, and brought him to his feet. "I'm out of patience. Gone. Talk or you're going off this ledge." Axiom-man dragged him toward it. Bleaken shot smoke at him, but one shot of blue energy against Bleaken's hands stopped the villain.

Axiom-man picked him up and dangled him over the ledge. The street was over ten stories below. Enough of a fall to kill him. *Am I ready to do that?* He realized what was about to happen, but he couldn't break. It was either one man's life or everyone else's left in the city. *No, don't kill. Save it. It's reserved for one man.* And even then, despite all the horrible things Redsaw had done, did he really have it in himself to see it through to the end? The end-end?

He turned his attention back to Bleaken.

"You fool," Bleaken said. "Heights are as much an issue for me as they are for you. What do you expect to do? Drop me?"

"Something like that."

"So I could what? Rise back up and really unleash upon you?"

"You're holding back?"

"Of course I'm holding back, you idiot. I am more now than I was before. Funny how these little gifts of ours work, isn't it? Seem to change over time as if some kind of evolution."

Axiom-man wasn't completely sure what Bleaken meant. Altering of powers? Axiom-man knew his own experience, knew the *surges*, but Bleaken seemed to be hinting at more of a mutation where a power changes rapidly and, possibly, into something else altogether. He just didn't know how to phrase the question as to how he had changed. Instead he said, "If he's controlling you, I can help."

"Do I really look like a guy who would yield control?" Bleaken grinned. "I'm a guy who works out deals."

"Right, so he's controlling you."

"No, moron. If you knew as much about me as you claim, you would know I could walk away at any time."

"What's your payday?"

"You."

CHAPTER SIXTEEN

WITH A VIOLENT jerk, Bleaken pulled Axiom-man over the ledge of the building. The two bodies spun and tumbled toward the ground, the pavement rushing up to meet them. Axiom-man kicked on the flight and slowed his descent, but with Bleaken's pull on him and his seeming use of gravity to his advantage, Axiom-man had to crank up the speed to counter the opposing pull.

Bleaken swiftly raised his hand and a plume of dark gray smoke poured out of his fingers, coating Axiom-man in a cloud of darkness. The dark lasted for about one second before flashes of red and orange blinked and flashed within the murk of smoke.

"Mind if I play?" Lady Fire swooped in out of the dark and shoved herself up against Axiom-man, taking him out through a cloud of smoke and into the open. Axiom-man looked down. They were a mere forty feet up, maybe a little less.

No sooner did Axiom-man return his gaze to Lady Fire did he see her hands come up and clamp on either side of his head. He had been here before and still had the burns to show for it.

Hoping his aura was enough protection, he brought his fingers up and clamped them around her wrists, using his ultra strength to force them away from his head. The moment he did that, fire poured out of her hands. Axiom-man let gravity take him as he let her go and dropped beneath the barrage of flames. He swooped in and grabbed her by the legs and hips and flew her straight at the Bank of Montreal building. Her body slammed against the concrete structure and her head bounced back against the concrete wall then lolled forward. He lowered her dazed form and dropped her on the ground before high-tailing it back up toward Bleaken.

Axiom-man plunged into the smoke, eyes alight, helping him to see. There was no firm physical form here. Where was Blea—

A bear hug from behind told Axiom-man exactly where Bleaken was. Grimacing, Axiom-man growled and jerked his elbows and arms outward, detaching himself from the man. He turned and faced him then shot a blast of eye beams in his direction. The blast hit Bleaken dead-on in the chest and sent him careening back into his own smoke.

A shrill whistle from below. When Axiom-man looked, Battle Bruiser was on the ground, looking up, removing his fingers from his mouth after he'd whistled.

Patience gone, Axiom-man moved as if to lower himself to land in front of Battle Bruiser to confront him. Instead, he lurched forward at the last moment and came down with both feet on top of Battle Bruiser's wide shoulders. The man crumpled beneath the impact. Axiom-man stood atop him for a moment to make his point, then hopped off. Bruiser groaned on the ground then, with the sleeve of his leather jacket, wiped the sweat off his forehead.

"Not bad, kid," Battle Bruiser said. He rolled over onto his side as if to get up. Axiom-man kicked him in the head, sending him rolling onto his back.

Axiom-man put one boot against the shoulder socket of Battle Bruiser's right arm, pinning him.

"You all seem to be in this together," Axiom-man said.

"In what?"

"Where is he?" Axiom-man said as calmly as possible.

Bruiser leaned over and spat on the ground. "Bleaken's up there, dumb face!"

"Where is—"

Bleaken struck from the side, this time without the aid of smoke. A sharp clunk made Axiom-man's head rattle, especially on the side by his eye. He lashed out in a reflexive kick only to miss his target and hit nothing but air.

A cloud of smoke surrounded his head. As if old practice, Axiom-man lit up his eyes then blasted into the dark. Normally, he wasn't one to shoot his eye beams willy nilly. But this was different. Any shot, even a lucky one, would be acceptable right now.

He didn't hear any reaction from Bleaken so probably missed.

Frustrated, Axiom-man pawed at the smoke, as if parting it would reveal his enemy. All it did was brush it away into the air and off into the mild wind.

A solid charlie horse to his thigh buckled his leg and his left foot angled out to the side.

Drawing his leg in slowly, fighting against the pain, Axiom-man raised his fists for whatever might come next.

Bruiser clocked him hard—first a hook to the shoulder, numbing the arm, then a shot from the opposite side across his cheekbone.

The sound came first . . . then the pain. Whatever Bruiser did broke the bone. Axiom-man just hoped it wasn't in a jigsaw puzzle beneath his flesh but maybe a crack or two instead. He dared not touch it right now in case he accidentally made it worse. Battle Bruiser wasn't playing games and the only thing the man understood when it came to combat was brute force.

Through the fog of a rattled mind and droning pain, Axiom-man forced himself to focus. *Stay current. Stay present. Find the shadow in the dar*—An uppercut shot his head backward, sending a bright shock of pain to the base of his neck.

Axiom-man interlocked his fingers behind his head then brought both fists down like a hammer. The moment the bottom of his palms struck Bruiser's hat then the top of his head beneath, Axiom-man knew he hit pay dirt. If he had put enough force behind the blow, it would have sent Bruiser's head crushing down on his vertebrae, if just for a moment, temporarily compressing the vertebrae, the discs, the spinal cord, and anything else beneath the skull.

All he heard was a surprised, "Opf." Then, righting himself, Bruiser stumbled back, arms partly out to the side at an angle, trying to maintain his balance. Without wasting a second, Axiom-man marched two steps toward him then gave him the hardest kick to the gut he could muster. Bruiser took the shot and bent slightly forward. Axiom-man brought in a haymaker with this right hand then followed it up with the same from his left. Battle Bruiser's head more or less now facing straight forward, the man completely dazed, Axiom-man shot out his fist and connected knuckle to teeth. He then brought in a hard left, first to Battle Bruiser's kidney then, from the right, another violent haymaker with a full body twist to add to the momentum to send the man down onto his hands and knees.

Axiom-man grabbed as much of the short dark hair at the back of Battle Bruiser's head as he could and torqued the man's head back. "Where is he!"

"Sky."

Sky. Always sky. Always . . . sky.

Then it clicked and Axiom-man knew why he couldn't find Redsaw.

THE SUMMONING

———

Oscar sat alone in his office, one leg crossed over the other, resting his elbows on his thighs, fingers loosely steepled together.

It had taken a long time. A very long time, by his standards, but perhaps not by most. He had brought himself out from poverty. He had tapped into smarts he didn't know he had. He had studied. He had learned. He had applied knowledge.

Money.

Locations.

Name recognition.

Favors.

Dealings that seemed above-board but occasionally dipped beneath the table.

His humanity fulfilled.

The black cloud.

That night.

The power.

The intent to save the city only to discover his power had a darkness to it that was formidable and difficult to fight. Eventually he gave in. He wasn't sure if his master helped with that or not, but what he did know was the world within the Doorway of Darkness was where his master dwelt. It was in that place of red and black clouds—the place of eternity in all directions—that he saw and felt the true nature of the power within him. He knew how to access it, but he suspected that he didn't know how to *fully* access it. He suspected his master was withholding or somehow holding him back.

There had to be a way for his master to give it all to him. Some way of asking for it or discreetly obtaining it.

But there was one problem. The Doorway was closed.

Yet, there in his own building, Oscar had access to a person who knew Axiom-man and, he figured, on a level that was more than just hero-saves-girl. But if that was all Valerie saw in him—a rescuer with power and nothing more—then there really was no bond and, as consequence, no leverage.

He would spy out Valerie's apartment. He would look for Axiom-man and see how often he came by.

He would learn . . . then he would act.

———

Axiom-man flew a perimeter around the city, his eyes peeled for Redsaw but this exercise was more for thinking than capturing. Should he see Valerie before finding Redsaw and facing him for what could be the final time?

"I could lose," he said quietly to himself. "He's always been more powerful." *But you've also beaten him in the past.* "That's not true. I *stopped* him, not *beat* him."

He wondered if not ending Redsaw's reign of death sooner had been a big mistake. Should he have been more diligent in locating the man in the black and red suit then ending him?

With the way the city was, all answers pointed to yes. He should have done a better job. People were dying, the city was physically crumbling, and the riots had started up anew. Below, people stormed the streets, some in take-back mode, marching down the roads, armed with whatever weapon they had access to—a baseball bat, a butcher's knife. The few who had a license for them carried firearms. Others took a shot at those attempting to maintain some sort of order, and others went for them in general for a pleasure beating or taking someone out with a bullet.

There was only one way to find Redsaw.

Axiom-man had the location.

Now he knew how to pinpoint it.

Chapter Seventeen

Using darkness as cover was such a cliché that Redsaw hated the very notion, but at the same time, he couldn't deny its usefulness as an ally. With his black mask, black cape, and large jagged portions of his suit in black, the aid of shadow came in handy despite the fact he didn't really need it. He was too powerful for anyone to be opposition anyway so whether coming out from the dark or just simply landing in front of his prey didn't really matter.

But he liked the sneak attack.

Liked the control. He could choose the moment to spring out. He could choose *when* a person would die. If he landed in front of them, he'd have to obey whatever rules came out of the confrontation, like ending the life before he had a chance to toy with it.

That guy over there, standing on the corner, ear buds in, grooving by his lonesome in awkward dance moves. He was lost in his own little world. Everyone was these days. If it wasn't tuning out the public world with music, it was tuning out the public world with whatever social app you had on your phone. People were easy pickings these days. Most walked around with their head down, glued to their device. A poor practice when out in public and especially downtown. But Redsaw—through Oscar Owen—knew people were sheep and did what they were told and were easily spooked and distracted.

Like that guy on the corner.

Half the city was being destroyed and all this guy could do to get away was pump up the jam and have a one-man party.

The sound of sirens rose on the air, and Redsaw recognized them as belonging to firetrucks.

The riots. The lootings. The fires.

All child's play.

And all a business deal except Redsaw's business was reopening the Doorway and dealing with his master without, hopefully, Axiom-man interference.

It began by drawing strength from random killings. Redsaw had gone all over the country, executing people. The random nature and random locations made it impossible for law enforcement to follow a pattern. He didn't use any powers that would leave a mark like a burn or something for forensics to discover. Just a slash of the throat, the squeezing of lungs until bursting, the removal of jaw bones from the skull . . . easy. And it worked. The streets grew restless due to the violence Redsaw inflicted to the bafflement of the police. Once the city was astir and wary, it took only one thousand dollars to get things started.

One thousand dollars. Nor more, no less.

The money went to a desperate meth user who belonged to a group of neo-Nazis. All the skinhead had to do in exchange was walk into the lower levels of The Empire and crack the bouncer guarding the area in the nose then walk out. The skinhead did it and, according to the papers, was found mutilated to shreds in a dumpster about a block away. Though the *Free Press* didn't name the killer, everyone who was anyone in the underworld knew the signature: Bleeders. Though the name sounding like a group of angry teens made it up, it meant much more. Everyone who crossed Tony Sterpanko was handed over to the Bleeders. The paper didn't name him, but those on the inside knew who the man he was seeking was because it was well known Tony spent his nights at the poker table with loose women and men he knew he could cheat.

Tony had been on Redsaw's hitlist at first. A powerful kill to make a statement. But, instead, using his business acumen, Redsaw decided to let the deadbeat live and, in return, create a war between the neo-Nazis and the Bleeders, a war which quickly escalated and spilled out from The Empire into the streets. Police came, guns were fired, cops and criminals died.

And the Bleeders had allies.

The Spokes, the Tormenters, the Headingly Skulls—all came to the rescue. Cops outnumbered, Axiom-man with his hands full.

Neo-Nazi bodies hung by ropes from streetlamps like the Christmas lights normally hanging off them come November and December. The layman threw stones. Others tried to jump up and grab the bodies and tug them down. No one had the reach but a stick with a flaming rag at the end did.

Firemen. Police. Paramedics. Even a small portion of the army all started working overtime. But it was too late.

Gangs were gangs, and while there was severe loyalty amongst its members and even through certain associations with competing gangs, all that went through the window when the civilians came out—random crooks—and started sneaking around the fights, busting open store windows, robbing what was within. Redsaw figured nearly every cash register downtown was empty, never mind how many ATMs were knocked over and beaten to a heap with sledgehammers until the cash fell out.

Redsaw stepped out of the shadows and slipped to another dark patch along the wall behind the guy dancing to the music. For a moment, the dude looked like he was in the middle of filming a music video: body grooving, fiery lights shining up against a smoke-filled sky, screams and sirens adding a grit to the overall performance.

Redsaw jumped out of the shadows and brought on the noise.

———————

Axiom-man floated above the city. Though it was a terrible thing to admit, he was now used to seeing the city this way—smoke, fires, ashy clouds, screams, shattering glass, sirens. It had been going on for so long the petty crime the city suffered before was completely serene by comparison. He had thought Winnipeg was in danger from simple crime when he first started. Then those with special abilities began to rise, Redsaw being the first after himself. That was when Winnipeg took on a new light. It wasn't a light caused by a certain power or ability. It was the shadow of darkness that rested on the streets. To the naked eye, the city was the city. People walking to and from work. People riding the bus. Some guy riding his bike, another person jogging down the sidewalk. Cars honking, the occasional shouting of a curse word, laughter from the outdoor patios at the pubs. All seemingly normal, your average Canadian city. But Axiom-man saw something else. All those things, those items that people considered part of the norm, were now exposed to dangers most people didn't know about. That was why when Redsaw first showed up, people were afraid. That's why when Bleaken appeared, people were taken by surprise, thinking Axiom-man had vanquished any further potential superpowered threat.

And even now, once again the city had been taken by surprise. Not everything Axiom-man did made the papers. Just the awe-inspiring feats that made good headlines and sold media. The news didn't get into crashing through the roof of a drug den and taking out crackheads while others too doped up on heroine were aware of what horrible things were being done to them but couldn't do anything about it. It also didn't talk about the semi-truck Axiom-man forced off the road with kids filling the entire trailer, some as young as three. The radio hosts and podcasters also didn't mention the time Axiom-man took a blade across his wrist while he stopped someone from doing the same to themselves. Fortunately, the slash only cut through the thick fabric of his glove. Had it been his skin, he would have bled out.

People liked the sunny stories. The ones where the champion stands atop a heap of enemies, bold gleaming sword in one hand, the other hand on the hip in victory, the cape billowing about behind him, tossed by a perfect wind that made it look ideal. They didn't want to hear the truth. Didn't want to know about how corrupt and off kilter the entire city was. This was why the riots and fights and all that damage took everyone by surprise. Panic induction. Fear. Human instinct lashing out in survival amongst the chaos.

"He's . . . I've got to find him," Axiom-man said. He scanned the skies. Gray rain clouds hovered over a city gripped by dark clouds of its own.

There was only one method to locate Redsaw and Axiom-man felt like a fool for not doing it before. Then again, it hadn't really been an option before. And even now it was still a shot in the dark—just a better shot.

Redsaw kept to the skies, if those who informed Axiom-man had told the truth. The smoke over the city and the clouds higher beyond were the perfect hiding place for someone controlling the disaster and leading the city into turmoil.

"And you were looking for a flying man on the ground," Axiom-man said. "So was everybody else." *The answer was right there and I missed it!* Yet, he realized, the sky was a vast place that made the city below nothing but a tiny map dot by comparison. However, Axiom-man did have his compass.

Himself.

———

Redsaw flew straight up, tossing the severed head to the side as he ascended but not before taking a bite out of the victim's cheek. Blood and death: keys to the Doorway. He knew the path. He'd traveled it before and the power beyond the door took his breath away. And now the Doorway was almost recreated, but this time on a scale that, if he used his past experience as a guide, could swallow Winnipeg whole.

All those beautiful black clouds could circulate and fill the place. His master would emerge. His power would grow beyond imagination or reason.

Fingers crackling with red energy, a rush and surge of sheer force pumping through him, Redsaw fought the extraordinarily overbearing temptation to start cutting into the fabric of molecular reality and begin opening the Doorway anew.

Last time, it took some effort done through a level of ignorance to get it open. Now he knew how to do it which was why he was waiting.

But he'd have to dispel some of the power blasting through his veins as things were at the brim and it was not yet time.

It was never time.
Not with Axiom-man still out there.
Not with him still alive.

———

Axiom-man barrelled through the sky, twisting and turning as he went into the rain clouds, moisture already beginning to soak through his uniform. The wind whipping past him as he flew only added to its chill, but at the same time flashes of heat swept over him as anxiety and caution went through his system.

He kept his eyes peeled, searching in all directions for two things: Redsaw himself or an indication of him. A wisp of black cloud would be enough to help narrow down Redsaw's location. But Axiom-man had the feeling he had no choice but to do this the way he didn't want: find the air path that would start to make him sick, start to make him feel like his powers were being pulled away.

It was like the first night with that black cloud all over again, the one that ultimately led to the creation of Redsaw.

This was the way to find him. All he needed was a starting point.

———

Redsaw soared into the clouds and buried himself deep within them. Surrounded by dewy mist, he paused mid-air and considered the next step in his plan. Most of the pawns were in place. The violence and blood in the streets were a testimony to their very presence, a testimony of people gone mad.

A strong surge of red power filtered through his veins and crackled in his fists.

He took in a slow deep breathe then exhaled just as slowly. *Keep it in, keep it contained.*

Through simple practice and time, Redsaw had taught himself how to better control the flow of power through his hands. He was not the same man that first showed up shortly after Axiom-man. He wasn't the same man who tried to be of help to people only to discover it was impossible. The red power had been tapped and it was then he learned its true nature: evil, fueled by darkness. Worse, it was a part of him. There was nothing he could do to remove himself from it. The night when the black cloud came and entered him, it stayed, using him to serve his master in the other realm. Time. Battles. Thought. The Doorway. Redsaw understood the thing had slowly overtaken him and turned him to its point of view.

And he agreed with it.

His master was unjustly chained to a realm of red and black clouds, bound by a barrier that forbade entrance into this world. But there was a danger. He learned it the night he first opened the Doorway of Darkness. *He* was just a pawn, chosen solely because he had the mental and inner fortitude to handle the red power and, eventually, grow strong enough to bring his master through the portal. But after that, once his master was free, Redsaw knew his purpose would be fulfilled and, unless there were any further assignments, he'd be removed either by the stripping of his powers or by the stripping of his life altogether.

He couldn't let that happen. Not with knowing Axiom-man's abilities were the key to ensuring he could overcome his master and remain alive, both his and Axiom-man's powers his own. But all this was hypothetical and Redsaw hated the hypothetical. He worked off facts, proven evidence, stats, confirmed and corroborated information, and any other method that would provide certainty for a decision. His thoroughness when it came to making choices was what made him as Oscar Owen so successful. Business wasn't hard if you educated yourself before making a choice. It really all boiled down to that.

Redsaw was in the same position now. He had a choice to make. Things needed to be conducted in order otherwise his doom would be sealed. Maybe not right away or tomorrow but one day. Opening the Doorway again was a requirement of his master and the black cloud within Redsaw could not help but obey.

The trick would be in what he would do once his master was out.

Chapter Eighteen

Axiom-man did his best to remain within the perimeter of the city, that was, all the way from the city proper into suburbia and stopping just before the rural boundary lines. If Redsaw was indeed up here, he would want to be near his handiwork, but no matter where Axiom-man flew, he could not pick up on any trail of the black cloud—of *any* black cloud—to help get him to the starting line to tracking down Redsaw.

He headed back in the direction of the city centre.

Valerie entered his mind. The poor girl. He knew he was being difficult, but not on purpose. His heart ached at the realization of his naivety and ignorance when it came to their relationship. He had gone about it all wrong, treated it as if he was just an ordinary boy dating an ordinary girl. Ordinary love. Ordinary romance. Ordinary friendship as the foundation.

He just hadn't factored in the Axiom-man element. He honestly thought the relationship would be your standard—or *better*—romantic relationship with all the love and wonderfulness that came with it. And those things did come and his heart swelled with joy at how well he and Valerie fit as a couple.

But that was Garbiel and Valerie. That was without the blue cape interfering. It was hard to keep getting up to leave because of some news report or an alert for keywords of tragedy he set up on his computer a long time ago. The cape . . . it was almost a novelty at first. Valerie was thrilled day after day to be dating both Gabriel and Axiom-man. She once confessed she had the best of both worlds, one based on a regular person and another based on someone who had ultra abilities. What neither of them expected was the blue cape becoming a slowly-developing wall between them.

Here, in the sky, the pang of loneliness hit Axiom-man's heart. He looked at his light blue gloves, grabbed a bunch of the fabric of his cape and gave it a squeeze. This suit, these powers, were intended for good. And while good was undeniably executed, each outing, each good deed, each flight was slowly breaking down his connection to Valerie. She'd been acting more distant recently. At first, he had chalked it up to stress at work and a busy mind. But he knew her too well and, whether she was doing it consciously or subconsciously, she was pulling away and Axiom-man knew the cape was the culprit.

He slowly shook his head at himself. *Did you really think it would be normal or, if not normal, then manageable?* "Yes, yes I did," he whispered.

Tears pricked the corners of his eyes . . . and a rush of nausea overtook him.

Red hands burned into his sides and pulled him downward.

———

It only took Axiom-man a moment to realize what was happening outside of the obvious. Redsaw had done this to him before: yanked him from the sky. The last time he had been flying with Valerie. Thankfully, now, she wasn't around.

Like a wolf spotting a deer, Axiom-man's mind went into battle mode.

He finally found him.

Axiom-man ignored the searing heat burning into his ankles and fired up the energy beams in his eyes and shot downward at Redsaw with everything he had. Redsaw released one leg and held up a hand, blasting back the blue energy with a fiery red shot of his own. The red struck Axiom-man in the eyes, momentarily blinding him . . . but it didn't matter. Redsaw still had hold of his foot so he knew exactly where he was. Axiom-man poured on the power again, firing hard at his enemy, his blue energy beams violently colliding with surges of red power, a sonic boom sounding as the two forces met with fury.

In the middle of the energy exchange, a dark purple wave of crackling electricity began to ballon out, growing wider and wider the more each dumped power against each other, each one fighting back with all they had.

Axiom-man's ankle howled with pain. If he let Redsaw hang on any longer, the man would burn clean through his ankle and remove his foot. Axiom-man jerked his leg upward with as much ultra strength as possible, bringing Redsaw up with it. Redsaw plowed into the ever-growing purple ball of energy, the shock of its power forcing him to ease back. Axiom-man didn't know what precisely caused the mild retreat or what the man in red and black was experiencing, but whatever it was, it helped. He supposed Redsaw entering the mix of both powers only amplified Axiom-man's force against him.

Finally. It was good to finally be the stronger of them. All those *surges* were about to pay off.

Redsaw released from the purple bubble the moment it exploded and lit up the sky, sending the two cloud warriors flying backward in opposite directions. Axiom-man flipped backward, head over heels, until he had the strength to counter the momentum and finally slow himself to a stop midair.

He scanned the distant clouds for Redsaw, searching for any sign of the man's presence. He didn't see anything. He quickly searched inside himself for any inkling of discomfort that would indicate Redsaw's presence.

Axiom-man was fine besides the sheer pain in his ankle. "Where are you?" He was going to find him, going to end him. He had to cross that line. He didn't want to. Knew it would change him, but he had no choice.

Not anymore.

———

Though everyone knew clouds were made of water and other particles, something common most forgot was water was a good conductor.

The clouds were the bathtub.

Redsaw was the toaster.

He slammed his hands together in a giant clap, dumping as much red power and energy into them as he could, the power building and building. He fought himself with as much restraint as possible to contain the energy until it begged to be let loose.

But he couldn't let it loose. Not here. Not now.

He needed the power for the Doorway. But he also needed Axiom-man dead for the Doorway.

There was no choice. With a grimace and a growl, Redsaw cut loose, sending a wild blast of red fiery energy into the clouds, lighting them up like lightning.

———

Energy hit Axiom-man from all sides, every angle as if caught in a bubble of pain. Red fire burst around him.

His insides sank. A splitting headache sent a shout through his head. His limbs locked and his stomach swam so thick with nausea, throwing up would be inevitable in the next two seconds.

He cut off his flight and let gravity take him with everything she had. His descent picked up speed as he fell from the clouds, his body slowly coming around to feeling more or less normal. Once a goodly distance away from that ashy red cloud, he kicked on the flight and soared beneath it, keeping enough of a distance so whatever was happening inside of it wouldn't affect him.

A black spot in the distance. One too tiny to be a plane.

Kicking it into high gear, Axiom-man flew as hard and as fast as he could muster. He crossed his forearms in front of his face for a shield.

Redsaw's form grew larger and larger the closer he neared.

Between the crosshairs of his forearms, Axiom-man fired from his eyes, the beams piercing into Redsaw while he closed in. Redsaw flew back, turned in the air, faced him. His arms drew up and Axiom-man summoned as much effort as possible to increase his speed. Before Redsaw could shoot out any opposing force, Axiom-man plowed into him, the bone of his forearms striking where Redsaw's ribs met his gut.

They smashed together and bone struck bone. Axiom-man hoped the position of his forearms slamming into the under curves of Redsaw's ribs would force the strike to crack Redsaw's lower rib bones like kindling.

A crack sounded in Axiom-man's ears, so did Redsaw's desperate, raspy gasp for air.

Take him! Axiom-man thought. He quickly flew behind Redsaw and wrapped his forearm good and tight against Redsaw's neck. Using his other hand to reinforce the effort, he squeezed the man in red and black tighter and tighter against him, doing everything possible to cut off his air.

Waves of achy sick pain coursed through him, the rims around his eye sockets aching as if hungover from a bad night out. Stomach swimming, Axiom-man focused his attention from discomfort to the agony in his ankle. If he could just concentrate on one thing in terms of an unavoidable distraction, that was it. It began to help as all attention of pain was focused on his ankle thus a distraction from the nausea.

He lit up his eyes and fired into the back of Redsaw's head. The man screeched and convulsed with every pulse of blue energy.

Somehow the man was able to take it, then Axiom-man saw why—black-gloved hands glowing slightly red pressed against the back of a black cowl.

The hands fired up and a burst of red energy forced Axiom-man to let go. What felt like a baseball bat slugged hard against his stomach, folding him in half like laundry over a line. Redsaw pulled his arm out from the fold, punched Axiom-man hard and downward, forcing Axiom-man to see nothing but the distant city below.

Ears ringing, Axiom-man twisted, balling his fist, and clocked Redsaw a solid one across the cheek. The man's head turned with the blow then snapped back.

"Not quite how you remember it, huh?" Redsaw said.

"No," Axiom-man said, fully straightening in the air then glancing downward. "It's pretty much exactly how I remember it."

"Touche."

128

"But you may be in for—" He was going to say, "A few surprises," but cut himself off. He didn't want Redsaw to know he had grown stronger since they last fought. Anything to have an edge in this, even the element of surprise, was most welcome.

"In for—?"

"This," Axiom-man whispered and fired everything he had at Redsaw, coating the man in the black cape in a halo of blue energy.

The man quaked inside the bubble, Axiom-man's power starting to make him smoke. Sharp bolds of red lightning shot out from Redsaw's hands in all directions like a static electricity ball. All began to grow purple, then darker and darker and darker.

———

If you fail me, you will die.

It was the master.

Redsaw could barely shake his head. He let out a weak, "No," then proceeded to cut through the energy bubble with knives of red power, breaking it open and dispersing it in all directions.

Not far away, Axiom-man hovered in the air, fists drawn. Redsaw flew at him, fast. He had to be careful. He didn't want to dispel too much red power otherwise he'd never be able to open the Doorway. Well, that wasn't true. If Axiom-man slightly depleted the battery, a few vicious murders would restore to full charge.

"Not that easily," Redsaw said and dove down, flying toward him. He launched shot after shot of fiery power, each blast of energy forcing Axiom-man's body to jerk and turn with each impact. Redsaw flew over him, grabbed him by the collar of his uniform, and bent him over at a ninety-degree angle, aiming him right for the ground. As they rocketed toward the earth, Redsaw sent fist after fist into Axiom-man's face and torso, striking anything breakable that he could.

Axiom-man was limp in his hand.

Defeated.

CHAPTER NINETEEN

ALL WAS DARK and there was nothing but heavy bursts of pounding consuming Axiom-man's head and body. Each blow came from somewhere in the shadows and he had no idea where to place his hands or how to move or what to do to avoid them. Each shot felt like getting clocked with a brick except he remained conscious after. Ribs aching from the blows, head a swirl of spaghetti thought, Axiom-man fired up his eye beams and shot in all directions.

Except . . . another shot. Another blow. Another spin of the brain and the profound sharp shock of getting socked in the eyes. He fired off more shots. The blue light didn't illuminate the dark or give him any sort of help in seeing what was going on.

A sharp sting rang through his middle ribs on the right side. All he saw in his mind's eye were a couple of tree branches snapping in two. The air came in with difficulty and already his lungs began to pound for deeper breaths and not the shallow ones he was able to afford them.

He fired again and again, hoping to hit something, anything—and that something-anything here in the sky was Redsaw.

Suddenly, a flash of white whipped across his face and a giant solid force slammed into the left side of his head.

He fired, weakly, then realized the stomach-churning acknowledgement he hadn't been firing his eye beams at all. He had only *thought* he had. That was why the blows kept coming.

Axiom-man focused, lit up his eyes, fired once more.

I need to see! Did he just hit something? Someone?

Air swelled around him, the wind coming up from underneath, indicating a fall. Barely able to concentrate enough to move his arms, he reached over the top of his body and felt around until his fingers found something about as thick and strong as the lower end of a baseball bat.

I better not be imagining this, he thought. Axiom-man took hold of the object and yanked. It had a hold on his suit. He pulled again, trying to loosen whatever it was that gripped him. Another flash of light and his ears hummed.

He didn't know where he was or what he was going to do.

———

The second Axiom-man squirmed and moved his hand was the second Redsaw punched him square on the button. He even went so far as lighting up his free hand and pressing his palm hard against Axiom-man's forehead, hoping the energy beam from his hand would fry Axiom-man's brain in his skull like a chicken carcass for stock.

The ground was roughly a hundred feet away. Like a sprinter wanting to finish strong, Redsaw dug deep and pushed himself to fly even faster.

Not long and Axiom-man's entire body would be jelly on the pavement.

———

The strong sense of a large object nearing took over Axiom-man's senses. He was going to hit something. He didn't know what but knew it was imminent. Unable to fully grasp the moment, unable to focus and put his attention to the matter at hand, the thought of Valerie crossed his mind and heart. He smiled beneath his mask, or, at least, thought he did.

Valerie.

"Rrrg." A pause. "Grugh."

Axiom-man suddenly had the sense of freedom all around him.

Something coming up fast and hard beneath him. He kicked on the flight and hoped to God Almighty he wasn't imagining it. He violently slowed his rapid descent, cutting the speed in half at first then, with another surge of effort, cut it in half again.

Tilt . . . your chin . . . to chest . . . to . . .

He hit the ground, back first, his last-second effort to keep his skull from striking whatever it was going to smash making it possible to retain its position upon first impact. A second later, the force that slammed against the entire back of his body made his head go back and bang . . . he wasn't sure.

The last thing he heard inside his head was the loud dull thunk of his skull hitting cement.

Redsaw was still in the air, Axiom-man somewhere below, hopefully dead. He wanted to confirm the kill. Nobody could survive a fall like that and he knew Axiom-man wasn't invincible unless the man had changed since their last encounter. Redsaw wanted to fly down, hit the street, see the mess of flesh and fabric and blood and potentially absorb Axiom-man's power.

But he couldn't.

He could barely see. Nothing but fog filled his vision and not from the clouds of smoke. He wiped his eyes in an effort to get rid of any tears blurring his vision but to no success. His eyes were dry.

Peering through a small slit in the black surrounding the top and bottom of his vision, Redsaw carefully lowered himself to an alley below. The moment he touched down, he stumbled and tripped over a garbage can. Pure fatigue and outright sleepiness consumed him. Something had struck him in his cheeks, puncturing the skin. That's what his tongue told him when he felt around inside his mouth. He felt the area, his fingers grazing over three tiny hard bumps on his skin. He put a couple fingers to one of them to feel it. It was a small protrusion, maybe only a couple millimeters above the skin line, hard like wood or metal. The other two felt the same.

Redsaw fell to his knees and the tiny slit of vision narrowed even more. His limbs felt like noodles and all he wanted to do was lie down for some shut-eye. He couldn't do it here. Not out in the open like this, not in uniform.

He fell against a dumpster, the sound of his crashing into it muted to tired ears.

"Gruah!" He smashed his fist into the side of the dumpster, denting it.

He slid down beside it and collapsed face first on the pavement. Try as he might to get up, he didn't have the strength. The ground became extremely comfortable and all he wanted was to just close his eyes for a few minutes and—

"Wake. Up," he said firmly to himself.

If you fail me, you will die. It was the master again.

Eyes now closed and still barely awake, Redsaw concentrated as best he could and floated up so he was level against the dumpster's lid. He felt around for the lid of the thing and had to rise a bit higher to locate it. Using what strength he could gather, he opened the lid just enough so he could squeeze through. He floated sideways, squeezing himself into the opening, dropped the lid and fell onto the putrid trash within.

———

Ears ringing, Axiom-man opened his eyes, his vision filled with a dark gray boot. It was on his chest, pinning him down.

"You . . . better . . . remove that," he said to whomever the boot belonged to. He couldn't move his head the pounding was so bad and he could barely see. A swish of dark gray cape brushed over his face when the person adjusted their footing, their boot still on his chest.

"All that power and look at you," the gray figure said.

"What do . . . what do you . . . mean?"

The boot pressed harder against his ribcage. "Your time is coming. And it will hurt and you will wish you never dawned that blue cape." The figure released their boot, planted it beside him next to the other foot, then turned and walked away, eventually blending with the smoke on the air.

"Wait . . ." Axiom-man said, reaching out a feeble hand for help. He dropped his arm when the figure was gone.

The ringing in his ears came down a level in volume, the sounds of the city's chaos slowly rising on the air.

Everything hurt from head to toe. Axiom-man was afraid to move. Any accidental wrong movement could result in permanent injury. He took a second, closed his eyes, and first focused his hearing on what was around him, checking for people. He didn't hear any murmuring voices nor the sound of shuffling footsteps nor any indication he was being watched. He opened his eyes and did his best to roll them around in their sockets to see if he noticed anything or anyone around him. So far as he could tell, he was indeed alone.

No one had seen the gray figure except for him.

Closing his eyes again, Axiom-man put his attention on his body. Arms felt intact and were laid out beside him, about a foot from his middle on either side. He checked his legs. His left was pretty much straight, foot flopped over to one side. His right, however, was partially angled inwards with his knee about three-quarters facing the pavement. The rest of his leg tilted in the same direction. The pain from the burn on his ankle was present but also distant as he tried to figure things out.

Good limbs first, he thought and wriggled his fingers and gently rotated his arms side to side, just enough to ensure they could in fact move. He tested his left leg, simply rolling it left to right while also making an effort to control his foot. Things were stiff but there was no sharp indication of pain to mark an injury that needed tending to. His right leg was next and it took him a moment to envision the anatomy of it before he attempted to carefully roll his leg straight so his kneecap faced upward. The adjustment was uncomfortable and came with a grunt, but once he settled his leg back on the ground, things felt better.

"Okay," he said while giving a large exhale. "How to move without breaking yourself."

He thought about using his arms and hands to help himself sit up but his muscles felt like jelly, so he doubted they'd be of use. If they would be, it'd be slow-going.

There was only one safe option and, right now, playing it safe had to be done because Redsaw was still out there. Axiom-man could not risk accidentally making himself ineffective against him. His stomach swam with the thought of his failure. He had him. In the sky. But he was outfought and, after what Redsaw tried, it was clear the madman would do whatever it took to end his life. Slowly, Axiom-man rose off the pavement, his body horizontal to the ground. Once he was high enough, he cautiously adjusted his small flight to bring himself vertical. His feet hovered about six inches from the ground, dangling like a dead man in a noose.

Slow. "Go slow," he said. Slowly, he lowered himself so his feet touched the ground, balls of the feet first before settling on his heels. He kept the flight on, not letting his full weight rest on his feet just yet. He took a few deep breaths to prime himself, then let the weight settle. On his left side, the sudden onset of gravity took over and he had to put some effort into keeping his foot planted to remain secure. His right side vibrated with aches and pains from the damage to his ankle. He could stand on it. Just needed to remind himself it was burned not broken. The bones were still secure.

He stood there amidst the smoke. Shouts and sirens were all around.

Redsaw was gone.

He had failed.

———

The next day, Valerie sat in her chair at the office, phone to her ear. Gabriel's number rang and rang until an automated voice message stated the inbox was full and to try again later.

It wasn't that she *expected* to reach him; she simply *hoped* she would.

She hadn't seen Gabriel this morning at home nor had she seen him last night. The news had stopped their constant coverage of the riots a long time ago. Now they simply touched base on it for an update or new development, the attention put on other news from around the world.

There was no mention of Axiom-man or Redsaw.

Valerie hit the internet and searched for the both of them, hoping to find a recent headline from any news source, even social media, just to get a glimpse as to where things were at. Any reports she found were news she'd already read. The only new material were a few posts by some bloggers offering their thoughts as to the state of Winnipeg and how the police do not have everything under control. Nothing in the posts suggested recent events involving Axiom-man or Redsaw. She even went so far as searching Gabriel's name, wondering if something happened and he had been smart enough to ditch the costume prior to seeking help or giving news or—she didn't care anymore. She just needed *something*—even an obituary. Every Gabriel Garrison that popped up in the search results were for Gabriel Garrisons she didn't know. Valerie found it slightly amusing there were so many people out there who shared his name. She didn't think it'd be that common. She typed in her own name to lighten the mood and had a few chuckles at the various Valerie Vaughans that turned up.

"Now to find a Valerie who is a doppelganger would be fun," she said quietly. She glanced to the stack of papers beside her computer then to the ones sitting on top of the inbox.

Work could wait.

THE SUMMONING

She needed a boost

———

Oscar had flown to his office after waking in the dumpster in his own vomit. He must have upchucked at one point then fell back asleep. And *asleep* was what it was. Thankfully, in a way. Whoever tagged him dosed him with a very strong tranquilizer and shut him down. Despite his powers, he was still human beneath it all and sleep was sleep. He didn't like that last part—still human. With all he could do, godhood would be a more apt term.

Oscar discarded the Redsaw suit in a small office closet and exchanged it for a white button-down with matching blue dress pants and jacket. He left the tie off but did sink his feet into a pair of dress shoes, black and shiny enough to draw attention but not shiny enough to be obnoxious.

Oscar's face was but an inch from his door. On the other side, Valerie tapped on keys and shuffled papers. She *was* a good assistant and she was a smart hire, but now . . .

Keeping his anger at bay through concentrated breaths in and out through his nose, Oscar knew what he had to do.

He could dawn his gear, come crashing through the office window and scare the hell out of her, feeding off her fear. But Redsaw and Oscar Owen had to remain as disconnected as possible and that included Redsaw showing up at an Owen office. However, there were plans to break that rule down the line but not just yet.

Oscar only had one choice. He would follow her home.

CHAPTER TWENTY

VALERIE KNOCKED ON Oscar Owen's door before leaving, seeing if the man had any last-minute items she needed to attend to. Her knocks were met with silence. She hadn't seen him come in but did hear him moving about his office. It wasn't uncommon for Mr. Owen to stay the night, working, and crashing on the office couch before doing it all over again the next day. The man was rich for a reason and hard work was one of those reasons.

She slung her purse over her shoulder, padded her pocket for her bus pass, then headed toward the door. The bus pass was always kept separate from the purse, the idea being if she forgot her purse somewhere, at least she'd still have a method of transportation instead of being completely stuck.

The bus ride home was long. Not that she lived terribly far away. It just seemed to drone on and on, her thoughts consumed with Gabriel, Axiom-man, Redsaw, and a city on fire. Though the windows of the bus were closed, she still smelled the smoke on the air.

She glanced around the bus. Approximately a dozen or so other riders were on with her. Gabriel taught her to keep an eye out for people. Look them over, check for anything that might be a potential threat, especially when traveling at night. Everyone she glanced at seemed all right. If there was any danger, it was concealed. Perhaps these folks simply wanted to get off the streets and moving around the city via bus was the safest way to do it? The fact the transit system kept skeletal transportation going said a lot about the city's determination to press through.

The thought of coming home to an empty apartment yet again made her heart sink.

Please be there, she thought. Yet, in the back of her mind, she wished he wouldn't be there at all.

———

Redsaw flew at a high distance from Valerie's bus. He knew she'd ultimately wind up at home and he could wait for her there, but on the off chance she got off the bus and met up with Axiom-man, if he was still alive, he had to be there.

Axiom-man needed to die.

———

Valerie turned on the light in her front landing, illuminating a portion of the dark apartment. She glanced around and didn't see anyone. She listened to the dark and heard nothing.

"What else is new?" she said, letting her purse slide off her shoulder and hit the floor.

She headed to the kitchen and flicked on the light. She squinted against its brightness for a second before her eyes adjusted and she headed to the fridge. A glass of orange juice and a splash of vodka would do the trick. She had a low tolerance for alcohol so even the equivalent of a shot was enough to relax her, make her sleepy and take the edge off her day.

She poured her glass of orange juice, leaving enough room to add the booze. As she went to the vodka cupboard, she heard a sloshing sound from out in the hall. She froze, listened, heard nothing. Heart picking up pace, she opened the cupboard, reached up, and grabbed the half-empty bottle of vodka.

The sound again. Like water.

She set the bottle down and carefully went to the kitchen's doorframe. She peeked out into the hallway and saw nothing.

The sound.

It came from the bathroom.

She looked at the bottom of the closed bathroom door and didn't see a light glowing from the bottom.

She felt her stomach. Was something sloshing in there, as silly as it was? Things felt all right so it wasn't that.

Valerie went back into the kitchen to finish preparing her drink when she heard the sound again. This time she marched straight out of the kitchen and stood by the bathroom door. A small *sloosh* came from the other side.

Should she say something? Was someone in there? Had someone broken in? Or . . .

"Gabriel?" she said just loud enough so she would be heard through the door.

Another slosh. She thought she heard a weak, "Val," but couldn't be certain.

Steeling herself, she took hold of the doorknob, gripped it tight, raised her other hand in a fist, and, "Three, two, one . . ." She shoved open the bathroom door. Gabriel lay in the tub, half in his costume, half out. She dropped her fist. What exposed skin she saw was beaten and bruised, mottled and red.

He could barely turn his head to face her. "Hi," he said softly.

She couldn't find the words. He wasn't dead otherwise he wouldn't be able to speak, but Gabriel was so bruised up the man was nothing but purple, green, and sickly yellow blotches with red blistered skin.

"Are you . . . how . . . ?" It was all she could say.

"Redsaw," he said, voice weak. "He's too strong." The water sloshed as he leaned in her direction. When he spoke, each set of words came out with a gasp. "It was almost over. I almost had him. But he got me. He got me." He looked her in the eye. "He got me, Val." He glanced down. "He got me."

It took a good minute before she could speak. "How long have you been lying in there?"

"I don't know."

She came over and felt the water. It was lukewarm. "You'll freeze if you stay in there."

"Might be good for the swelling."

"Was it cold or hot when you got in?"

"Got in." He grinned just a bit. "Fell in is more like it. He took me to the ground. Almost made me a hamburger patty on the cement."

A jolt shot through her. "What?"

"He almost killed me. Then someone . . . I've seen them . . . before. Gray. No . . . name. Somehow . . . stopped . . . Redsaw."

"Gabriel, you've got to get out of there." She moved toward him.

"Careful," he said. "Be careful. Gentle." After a pause, "Please?"

She nodded and grabbed his robe from behind the door and a towel off the rack. She came over to him. "How do you want to do this?"

"Only one way," he said. His eyes went blue and his hair changed color. The water sloshed as he rose from it, his whole body dripping as he cleared the top of the tub and adjusted himself so as to land on his feet.

He stumbled into her. All she could do was put his robe around him and place the towel on his head. She took a corner of the towel and very carefully and gently patted his face in an effort to help dry him. He took her hand in his, stopping her. Had she pressed too hard? Did she hurt him?

Gabriel held her hand, kissed her fingers, and powered down.

"You can't keep doing this," she said.

He gave her fingers a soft squeeze. "I have to finish this. He's planning something. He has the city."

"But he doesn't have me," she said. Valerie hoped he knew what she meant by that.

"Don't ever . . . if it ever happens . . . don't let . . . let him get near you. Or . . . anyone. It's too . . . too . . ." His knees buckled but he caught himself and stood straight again.

"Shhh," she said. "Let's get you to bed, okay? A rest will help. I'll get you some ice and some Tylenol. We'll make sure you're comfortable . . ."

His eyes went soft and glazed over. "I know . . . this is hard. Please . . . help me finish . . . this. We can . . . recover later. Talk later."

Despite not wanting any more of this metahuman stuff, she still nodded and adjusted his robe so he was fully covered and straightened the towel draped over his head.

A violent crash of glass filled the next room.

Valerie ran out of the bathroom. She heard a thudding footstep behind her, as if Gabriel was trying to slowly follow her. Before she could fully take in the broken balcony window, a black glove wrapped around her throat, the other raised with its palm close to her face. Red swirls of miniature lightning danced up and down the fingers. She tried to look past the palm but it was so close to her face she couldn't see beyond it.

And she didn't have to.

The voice that came from behind the hand sent a haunting chill into her heart. "Where is he?"

"Where's—" *Oh no. He knows. He knows! Gabriel!* She wanted to shout his name, tell him to transform, tell him to fly out and knock this guy hard. But she didn't have to. She peered to her left and Gabriel stood just outside the bathroom door, robe on, his face mostly concealed by the towel.

Redsaw snapped a finger at him. "Get back in there and close the door."

Gabriel seemed to hesitate. Was he seriously considering maintaining the double identity stuff right now? What was the matter with him? This was no time for glasses and stumbling into chairs and tables.

Can he help me? she wondered. *Or is he too . . .*

Gabriel started toward them. His movement was slow but nothing that would betray his condition. She searched the shadows beneath the towel covering his head, looking for any sign of crackling blue, energy-filled eyes. So far as she could tell, his powers weren't activated. Was he serious? Or was this meant to be some sort of surprise attack?

"Don't come closer," Redsaw told him firmly. To Valerie: "Where is he! I know he comes here but I can't sense him."

She inadvertently glanced toward Gabriel.

"A naked man in a bathrobe is your hope? Honey, you have no idea of the difference between who holds your life in his hands and who's standing there as some cheap boyfriend. What are you? A two-timer? One guy for power, another for . . . mediocrity? Where is he?"

No, you *have no idea of the difference of the man standing there and what he really is.* She gave Gabriel a stern look and a small, sharp nod. *Come on! Change!*

Redsaw squeezed her throat tighter. The air came in thin ribbons of oxygen. She could barely speak. "Gabriel . . . please . . ."

The man in the black cape turned to him as if considering him for a moment. "Your boyfriend can't do anything. If he moves, I will kill him."

Heart racing, Redsaw's fingers squeezing even harder against her throat, she waited for Gabriel to come to her rescue.

"Let . . . let her go," Gabriel said.

Finally. *You're about to receive some hell, buddy.*

Redsaw sent a blast of red energy across the room and blew Gabriel against the drywall, cracking it. Gabriel fell and collapsed on the ground.

"Gabr—" She had to cough, needed some air, but couldn't grasp a breath.

Redsaw's palm alit with red flame. "He will come to us."

When Gabriel came to on the floor, it took him a moment to acknowledge he was indeed face down, body beaten and bruised all over. He forced himself to look up to where Valerie had been.

Squeezing his eyes shut, tears running from the corners, Gabriel brought his fist to his mouth and bit down on it to contain his scream.

Both Valerie and Redsaw were gone.

Chapter Twenty-One

Immediately, Valerie had flashbacks to when she had been kidnapped the time Bleaken had clouded the city. She just had to remember to stay calm.

Oh, who was she kidding? Her heart beat like a banshee on drums and she could hardly take a full breath through the panic.

She glanced up at the man who had his heated hand around her waist, taking her through the sky.

Gabriel hadn't stopped him. Gabriel hadn't transformed. Gabriel . . . had let him take her.

She just didn't know where they were going.

———

Gabriel sat on the floor of his bedroom, back against the mattress, feet splayed out before him, slumped over. Every time he straightened himself, he couldn't help but sink back down. The man had Valerie . . . and he hadn't stopped him.

But he had to let him take her. It was all he could do. He was the only one standing between Redsaw, Valerie, and the rest of the city. If he had *shifted* and let the power out, given his condition, he would have surely been defeated. He couldn't imagine landing a single blow on Redsaw and he didn't want Valerie caught in the crossfire between energy beams in such a small space. Gabriel was fully aware Valerie was probably confused, angry, frustrated, worried, and deathly afraid right now.

If she was still alive.

Redsaw was killing and she could very well have been his latest victim. No, he couldn't think like that. She had to be alive. Had to be. But even if she wasn't, it didn't change the fact Redsaw needed to be stopped.

Worst thing was, the man in red and black could be anywhere.

Outside of hitting the skies again, there was only one other way Gabriel could think of that might help him track the man down: Jack Gunn.

————

Gunn sat slumped in his raggedy office chair, an old La-Z-Boy completely worn out at the seat. His head was dipped toward his chest, a bottle of whiskey dangled between his fingers of his left hand hanging over the armrest. He wasn't asleep. Just in a stupor.

Nothing is working, he thought. His forces barely kept up with the chaos, and while headway was being made to arrest those acting up and breaking the law, the real pain was the city showing its true self throughout this. Winnipeg had been a relatively peaceful place. Like all cities, there was corruption and crime bubbling beneath the surface, but despite the work to keep things from spilling over, it was manageable. After the gang war broke out, Gunn knew it would quickly escalate to a battle between all gangs willing to step up to the plate and assert new claims on merchandise and territory. Throw in a bunch of superpowered lunatics and you've got a powder keg.

And Redsaw's the match. Axiom-man had failed to track down the killer. At least so far as Axiom-man dragging Redsaw's body in front of him and handing him over. Dead would be ideal but knowing Axiom-man, he'd probably keep the murderer alive. The problem was, no facility could contain Redsaw even if they did catch him. He'd have to be under guard twenty-four-seven, the guards authorized to use lethal force if necessary. Someone, somehow had to keep Redsaw from using his powers to escape. There was the potential of gassing him and rendering him unconscious. But he'd have to be *kept* unconscious.

Gunn considered making a call to a surgeon he knew to ask about inducing a coma. He also knew that that may or may not work, depending on if Redsaw's body had the ability to combat forced sleep. Not that being in a coma was sleeping . . . but similar. But then what? Keep the man alive but unconscious until he died? *If* he could die?

Gunn tried raising the bottle to his lips but was so tanked already, he barely had the strength to move it so he let it hang.

Moments passed and a loud shatter of glass jolted him from his stupor. He didn't recall dropping the bottle.

"Wake up," a male voice said.

Gunn opened his eyes as best he could and grimaced when light blue fabric greeted him. He made a sweeping motion with his fingers to shoo him off but instead those same fingers were gripped, pulled, and he was yanked forward in his chair and fell to the floor.

"Get up," Axiom-man said.

"Kinda hard right now, pal," Gunn said, pushing himself upright.

"Then sit and listen." Axiom-man's glowing eyes filled his own. "I found him."

Gunn arched an eyebrow.

"But I didn't beat him."

How could Axiom-man say that so confidently as if it was some kind of achievement?

"What else is new?" Gunn mumbled.

"He had kept to the skies to stay off radar. I found him there. We fought. He's strong, and I'm glad your men hadn't the opportunity to engage, otherwise they would all be dead."

Gunn twirled a finger in the air. "Yay."

Axiom-man put a couple fingers under Gunn's chin and forced the man's head upward. "I need to find him again."

"I'm not a counsellor. I don't cover needs."

"You're drunk and I need you to concentrate. Shove the fuzz aside and focus. What can you tell me that might help me quickly locate him?"

"Do you think he texts me and lets me know where he is?"

"Gunn!"

"Wall." Gunn pointed a weak finger to a partially lit corner of the room.

Axiom-man went over, found another lamp, and turned it on. It was a map of the city, covered in red, black, blue, and green marker, lines crisscrossing this way and that, a few thumbtacks and some string along with a few pictures of guys with stares that would make a man freeze, and some newspaper clippings.

"This is a mess, Jack," he said. "All I see is nonsense."

"Look closer."

———

Axiom-man studied the map. "I don't see anything obvious."

"Are you blind!"

With a frown, Axiom-man turned back to the map. There were no blatant commonalities nor obvious convergences of locations. Then he realized what he was looking at. It wasn't a map. It was a record, a way to keep track of everything that was happening. The downside was, outside of a few markings with a red R, there was no information on the map that he didn't already know besides a few occurrences that must have happened while he was attending to other matters.

History repeats itself, he thought. *This isn't a crystal ball. You won't find—* He noticed a series of asterisks in gold marker Xed out randomly throughout the city.

"What's the gold?" Axiom-man said.

"Starting points. First clashes. At least . . ." Gunn hacked up a lung. It took him a moment to get his breath together to speak again. "At least that's where we think each one started. No shape or pattern."

Axiom-man crossed his arms. "No, not visually, but . . ." He reviewed each gold asterisk, each one tagged with a letter in black ink. Each letter was short for a gang name. Axiom-man reviewed his reasoning before speaking. "It started with the neo-Nazis and Bleeders."

"So?"

If Gunn was sober, the guy would catch on.

"Those are the two most known, powerful gangs in the city."

"Power struggle. What else is new? They do it all the time."

"Yeah," Axiom-man said, "but when have they ever brought it so wide out in the open that it created a ripple effect to the other gangs."

"Your point?"

"Assuming Redsaw incited the gang war, it was done strategically."

"So the maniac has a method."

"Which makes him dangerous. Powerful is one thing. Smart and powerful is another. He started with the top two gangs to make a point."

"You're starting into speculation territory, *detective*."

Axiom-man ignored the sarcastic remark. "Two points. One, he asserted his control over the gangs by demonstrating to the others he could get the top two to fight each other in a blood battle to the death."

"Not everybody is dead."

"No, but he created an example. He indirectly informed the smaller operations to rise up and do the same." Axiom-man traced a finger from one X to the next in the order he remembered the gangs starting up their fights. There was no pattern to the layout of the Xes but that wasn't the point. "He got everybody fighting. The lesser guys would more or less take care of each other all the while causing chaos for everybody else. Those in the middle are probably right now deciding if they should call it quits and retain what they have, cut their losses or go all out until the bitter end."

"And the second point?"

"Is another version of the first. He made a statement of consolidation. Redsaw showed he could put people on and off the board whenever he wanted. This would confuse the gangs because anyone they were in competition with would become unpredictable in their actions because Redsaw would manipulate them to do random acts."

"You're speculating again, Sherlock."

"I'm theorizing and it holds up. You know the gangs. You know what it's like on the streets. You know the difference between a gang skirmish and an actual gang war." Axiom-man scanned the newspaper clippings which were mostly headlines of either gang fights or fire outbreaks or a mass death. "The dates on these papers ebb and flow."

"They were only picked as thought pertinent at the time."

"But you also inadvertently confirmed what I just said. The dates suggest a sudden aggression that lasted for a time, then a regression. Typically revenge battles take place on a smaller scale, usually isolated incidents. Stuff your guys are used to. But this . . . it appears the battles were constantly rebooted. One would start, flow, someone would recede, and it'd die down. Shortly after, it would start up violent again, which means interference."

"You think he's winding them up like those creepy walking toy dolls?"

"I think he's keeping the violence going to feed whatever it is he is doing."

"And what is he doing?"

"I don't know, but we can use the ebb and flow to find out."

"I need a nap."

The man was pretty drunk. No amount of coffee in the world would bring him out of it. "Sleep it off but not too long. Get your guys to find out where things are dying down. Try to find out where things have gone quiet. That'll be our starting point." He waited for a response. "Gunn?"

The man snored.

———

Valerie winced against the rough rope tight against her wrists. She felt the bonds that kept her hands tied behind the small boiler furnace in some old storage basement somewhere. From what she could discern by touch, the ropes were probably a good half inch thick and tied so tight there was no way she could wiggle her way out.

Redsaw stood facing the aged brick wall in front of him, his black cape and cowl making him look like the Grim Reaper from behind.

"What do you want?" she asked.

The man waited a moment before speaking. "Why do you ask such clichéd questions?" He peeked over his shoulder. "Not surprising, by the way. Your generation is all video games and social media. You wouldn't know an original thought if it jumped up with a big sign in front of you."

Little does he know. Maybe I should play the stupid card here. After all—He turned and faced her and immediately her body went ridged. Though half his face was covered by his mask, the lower half that was exposed said it all: He was going to kill her.

Redsaw spread his cape along his sides then clasped his hands behind his back. "I'm not one for pleasantries."

Yeah, no sh—

"After all, what are they but a preamble to what is actually going to happen? It appears you humans have this need to wade yourself slowly into the deep end, always holding back, never really getting to the heart of anything. Humans" —he grimaced— "are beyond the point of cowardice. I mean, why face the truth when a smoothed-over explanation can be had instead?"

"Humans?" She didn't mean to say it out loud. *He's talking as if he's not . . . human. Isn't he like Gabriel? Just someone who can do things other people can't?*

"Humans." He didn't say anything further and came up to her. He bent down and put his face close to hers. Valerie noticed he neither inhaled nor exhaled. Maybe he wasn't human? His voice . . . low, filled with a sharpness that can only be attributed to distaste. He drew in even closer, his skin nearly brushing against hers.

There was still no air.

Valerie's heart thudded hard, and try as she might to talk herself down, Redsaw's eyes boring into hers forbade that. His facial muscles didn't budge. There was no expression except for a taught mouth and the mild formings of a snarl. She didn't know if she should speak or stay quiet.

She peered at his mask, trying to discern what kind of face might lurk beneath it. Something scarred? Burned? Just a random face in the crowd? Whatever he looked like under there didn't matter. He had her trapped and there was nothing she could do about it.

Redsaw kept his face next to hers.

He stayed like that for nearly an hour, maintaining the whole time. All Valerie could do was stare straight ahead and do her best not to panic.

———

Every step as Gabriel paced his apartment was pure agony. Every muscle along his posterior chain was stiff as a rock and as sore as a burning bruise. The steps were slow, barely a few inches at a time, but it was movement. Going to see Gunn took a special kind of focus, the kind where he forced himself to move as minimally but as fluidly as possible. Now Gabriel paid the price for heading out when he should have been resting. But he couldn't rest. Not until Valerie was safe. He tried laying down, tried sleeping or even dozing, but all he could do was lay there with a bombardment of thoughts of every possible worst thing Redsaw could be doing to her at this very moment.

If Redsaw had kept her alive.

He hadn't sensed the man's oncoming presence, and even though Redsaw blew into the apartment with potentially enough time for his whereabouts to remain unknown, he hadn't sensed Redsaw because his powers weren't activated. It was only when the energy flowed through him that he became aware of the man's presence and, as proven, Redsaw only sensed him when his powers were on.

He was in no condition to fight and though he could have transformed and made an attempt, he would have lost and Redsaw would know for certain Valerie's man-in-the-towel was Axiom-man. If he had known this, it could have greatly affected how he treated her and even how he dealt with Gabriel.

"It was a terrible decision," Gabriel said, grunting back the pain as he paced. "But it was also the right choice." *Come on, Val. Be strong. I have to believe you're still out there and still breathing.* "I will find you."

Gabriel slowly turned around and paced in the opposite direction. He glanced up at the ceiling. "Can you hear me?" He wasn't talking to God. "Usually how it goes is I plead for help then you decide if the situation is worth it." It was the messenger he wanted. "Clearly, you must know what's going on. You always seem to be aware. Why you don't step in—especially now with an entire city under siege—I don't understand. I thought we were in this together, but . . . I'm learning that's both true and not true." *He has my back but I'm the one doing all the work.* "Hmph." *Some partnership. Basically, one supervisor just watching while the worker gets things done.* "Short end of the stick." The messenger had healed him before, a long time ago, but Gabriel couldn't help but wonder if the messenger's current silence and inaction was because that was then and this was now and he'd come a long way as Axiom-man compared to that first time he desperately needed a healing touch.

Gabriel winced when his lower back locked up for a second then slowly released. "I don't think I'm going to have a choice but to wait this out." The anger furrowed his brow and scrunched his face. He clenched his fists and ground his teeth. This was completely unfair . . . but seemingly necessary.

He *shifted* and let out a small blast of blue energy into the ceiling, busting a hole in it but not clean through to the floor of the apartment above.

He powered down.

Slowly, like an old man paying the price after a heavy day of moving boxes, Gabriel headed toward the bed. Once he lay on the mattress and the stinging from the bruises subsided, he closed his eyes and did his best to clear his mind to nothing but a black blank screen, audio off.

Focus on the nothing. Focus on the nothing. Just let yourself drift. A mental picture of Redsaw grew in his mind's eye. *No!* He pushed it away and banished his headspace back into the dark.

He adjusted himself on the mattress and caught a whiff of Valerie's scent from the space beside him. Women always smelled so pretty. His heart ached when her face filled his mind's eye. *I'm sorry, kiddo. I have to put you aside. Have to concentrate.* He pulled the shadows from the right side of the vision and covered her over in black.

Just focus on the dark. Focus on the black.

Let it go.

Just . . . let it go.

CHAPTER TWENTY-TWO

Four. Days. Passed.

The metallic scent of tin wafted into Valerie's nostrils. Her head was bowed, still bound to the boiler. Prolonged exposure to its heat made every inch of her clothes stick to her body like packing tape folded against itself. She opened her eyes. The circular rim of a metal cup of water was right by her lips. The man hadn't given her a thing to eat or much to drink since taking her. Between the sweat and the panic, she'd give anything to slug the entire cup back, but to what end? Give him the satisfaction of keeping her alive while he moved about the room, lost in some kind of trance as if communicating with something only he could hear.

Probably all the demons inside him, she thought.

The water.

The interior of her mouth was sticky dry, and she hardly had any spit left to moisturize it. If she died on him, she wouldn't be of use as leverage against Axiom-man.

Against Gabriel.

"Live or die, the outcome is the same," he said.

"Why . . ." It was hard to speak from such a dry mouth. "Why keep me here? What's the point?"

He seemed to consider the answer and when he spoke, his tone was nonchalant. "Death."

It didn't add up. How would her death benefit him other than to, from his side of things, potentially drive Axiom-man into a frenzy, maybe create a scenario where Axiom-man would mess up and Redsaw would win. Yet, the man in the black cape was clearly more intelligent than most. There had to be an ulterior motive. The problem was, Valerie didn't know how to find out without flat-out asking which could then lead to further problems.

Best bet is to shut up and wait for Gabriel. You have to trust he knows what he is doing even if you don't. This is his world, his realm. She let out a small, frustrated breath through her nose. You don't understand their world. *You try, but you don't. Half-knowledge at best, maybe. Gabriel knows how this works. He knows Redsaw. He loves me. You need to trust him. You need to*—Instinct took over and she put her lips to the rim of the metal cup the second she felt its touch. Redsaw slowly poured water into her mouth, about a couple tablespoons by Valerie's estimate. He quickly pulled the cup away. Valerie let her eyes close as she first let the dry skin in her mouth absorb some of the water before swallowing.

He gave her a touch more, but only a tiny sip. A tease. Nothing satisfying.

Redsaw moved away from her, tossed the cup aside, spilling the remainder of the water, and looked upward.

He stayed like that for an hour while Valerie looked at the thin puddle on the cement floor.

Something was happening.

———

Gunn burped when he put his mouth to the receiver. He didn't mean to but it just came out. Tasted like orange juice and beer.

"You need to apologize," the captain said on the other end.

"Sorry, sir. Was an accident."

"You're an accident."

Gunn spat on his office floor. "Something I can do for you, Captain?"

"You were given an assignment and it is still ongoing. You haven't filed a single report nor have you kept me and my men updated with anything you're doing."

"Oh, hogwash. I've been sending reports since, I don't know, since you asked." He glanced at his computer. "I think."

"Think? Think nothing. I've got nothing. This has to stop. We're out of control and soon we're going to be borrowing officers from all over the country to help, never mind the blasted army coming through here. Most of the people have left, anyone who's stayed won't leave their home barring a scant few. Local economy is basically gone and our leaders in the Legislature are holed up in there good and tight as they spend their time dealing with Ottawa's inquiries and demands for resolution." The captain coughed. "This is *your* area, Jack. Get it done. I want every metahuman dead in forty-eight hours. If I so much as get a glimpse of a whack job in a costume, I will open fire on them myself."

You try beating these guys with limited resources. It's like taking a .22 to a tank. Good luck. "Understood. I'll do what I can."

"You better. Job's over—*over*—if you don't come through. Get my meaning?"

Gunn sighed. "Yes, sir."

The captain hung up, no good bye.

Gunn grabbed the can of beer off his desk and took it to the window. It'd probably been sitting there for days and was flat as heck but he didn't care. He took a sip and stared out the window. There hadn't been a sign or report from Axiom-man since his visit some days back.

THE SUMMONING

"You better be alive," Gunn said and left the can on the window sill.

———

Redsaw had allowed Valerie one full cup of water yesterday. It wasn't nearly enough but more than enough compared to what she had been getting. She could only surmise he was restoring a small portion of her strength to keep her going.

Why? Why was her being alive so important? Other than bait, she couldn't think of anything else.

She could barely stand when Redsaw had her arm over his shoulder and dragged her up a long series of stairs. Valerie didn't know where they were going other than up. Through tired and squinted eyes, she watched each tiled stair move past.

"Where . . ." She couldn't speak. Her mouth was too dry.

"Home," Redsaw said.

He's taking me home? I don't live upstairs. I live downstairs. I live downtown. Yeah, downtown downstairs. The thoughts weren't quite there but Valerie did her best to piece her own reflections together enough to speak to herself. Her heart was long past the point of rapid panic, the muscle probably too weak and fatigued to thud any faster. *Gabriel . . . hurry.*

If this was it. If, after whatever Redsaw was planning occurred, and she died—she didn't like the idea but was okay with it enough that if it needed to happen, she would allow it and let Death take her.

But all those you'll leave behind. What about Mom and Dad. Axiom-man. What about Axiom-man. What about

Axiom-Gabriel? Gabriel-man. What about . . . "Him?" she mouthed the word.

There was a loud creak and Redsaw pushed her through a door. She landed on her stomach, arms barely absorbing the blow of the fall. She may or may not have hit her nose. She couldn't tell at this point. She touched her face and felt a little bit of moisture beneath her nostrils. It seemed red against the skin of her fingers but it was so hard to see. She rolled onto her back. The night sky was masked with a thin layer of smoke, a gray murk that stunk of campfire and burning rubber.

It was so dark up here. If only she could see, she could—In her peripheral something bright and gleaming caught her eye. She lolled her head to the side for a better look and a band of silver coated her sight top to bottom. Valerie squeezed her eyes shut, gently rubbed each one with one hand, then opened her eyes again. Things were a little clearer now.

Redsaw was to her left, flying around a tall pole-like structure shrouded in a black tarp or cloth of some kind. But beside her was a tower of silver. Was it real? How could it be? How could anyone afford a tower of silver that was about fifteen or twenty feet high and at least three or four feet wide, some kind of giant cylinder that sharpened to a jagged peak.

Something big and black came down at the corner of her eye. Redsaw had finished unveiling another tower.

Valerie glance around the roof. There were three more towers covered in black.

This couldn't be good.

————

THE SUMMONING

Gabriel peered over his shoulder in the bathroom mirror, towel about his waist. His entire back up to his shoulders, his neck, the backs of his arms, and when he tugged the towel down a bit, his entire backside was covered in green and purple and jaundice yellow. He had a face half that of Freddy Krueger.

The long hot shower had helped relax things, which was the simple goal of the effort.

Gabriel headed to the living room, sat on the floor and put both legs out in front of him. Slowly, he leaned forward and reached for his toes. He could hardly bend without it hurting but things were better than when they originally happened. Breathing out and relaxing as best he could, he stretched his fingers toward his toes and held on by the tips once they found purchase.

"Slow," he said with a bit of a groan. He stretched forward, the focus being to relieve the stiffness in the muscles and keep things mobile. Any more resting and he'd run the risk of a real lock-up. His pacing had improved too. Though the messenger never responded to his inquiries, he had managed to improve his steps day by day, eventually obtaining a slow walk.

Gabriel slowly eased back off the stretch. The effort already caused a gleam of sweat to coat his skin.

"And forward," he said, breathing out. He held the stretch again, doing his best to be as relaxed as possible because any tensing caused a sharp pain in whatever muscle tightened up. But he couldn't help but tense up. Valerie's life was on the line and he had to hurry, get well as quickly as possible, or, at least, well enough to have a chance.

Leaning back, he caught his breath and slowly stood. A head rush greeted him upon becoming vertical. He put a hand a couple feet from his face and focused on it until the swoon passed.

Gabriel paced again.

———

"I reckon this one's a keeper," the big man said.

Valerie glanced up to a man in a black domino mask and a handlebar moustache. A woman in a black cowl colored like a reverse ladybug stepped up beside him. "Indeed. At least according to him." Valerie could tell she wasn't talking about the giant man.

Head fuzzy, she wanted to know why she was so important. She had nothing to contribute to what was going on other than some kind of leverage against Gabriel. *Axiom-man,* she corrected herself. *You can't . . . not with your head like this . . . you can't think of Gabriel. You have to think of Axiom-man and call him that and envision him as that. Don't run the risk of accidentally saying his real name. You can do at least that much for him.*

When she drew out of her rumination, the masked couple was gone.

Everyone was gone, including the roof.

Surrounded by darkness, a voice spoke to her. "Shadows come and never leave. Though the sun may shine, shadows always remain. I am shadow."

A haunting face graced the dark, shadowed by a hood, angry. Bleaken.

Then the black smoke lifted and Redsaw had unveiled the final silver tower.

Redsaw stood on the building's ledge, looking out at the city. At least, that's what Valerie presumed he was doing.

The man never moved.

THE SUMMONING

Gabriel had done all he could to help speed his healing along. He made sure to eat completely clean, loading in the protein for the muscles and vitamins from fruits and vegetables. He supplemented, and though the imbibement had only been after Valerie had been taken, he hoped it was enough time for his body to absorb and use what it needed to help make him more functional.

Sirens constantly rose and fell on the air and he so badly wanted to get out there to help, but he had to run the risk of letting things slide and people getting hurt if he was going to put an end to the madness once and for all.

"I have to kill him," he said, this time louder than the last time he spoke it an hour ago. It was a mantra. Every hour on the hour he had his phone set to beep to remind him to say it. It had been difficult at first, the thought of taking another life despite how despicable Redsaw was and how unworthy the man was to live, but killing was killing no matter how you looked at it.

Murder was murder.

He knew he walked the thin line again. A long time ago, thinking about killing Redsaw got him into trouble with the messenger. But given what was going on, he steeled himself against any potential conflict with the messenger over the issue.

It was the right choice to make.

"I have to kill him."

The two other costumed men and the woman had left the roof about an hour ago. To go where, Valerie didn't know.

Redsaw still didn't move.

———

It took nearly every cent in the bank and every hidden connection to make it happen, but Redsaw had secured his silver. What the public didn't know was that outside of material assets, Oscar Owen was broke. But it didn't matter. Not anymore.

Gods did not need money.

As he looked out over the city, he envisioned all the bodies and blood. Though he was responsible for many of their deaths, he wasn't responsible for all. But, as he had bled out an elderly man behind Johnny G's, he noticed a crackle of red energy snap from his fingers, drift along the air to the man, graze him, then crackle back.

It was then he understood what the master had just shown him.

———

Gabriel lay in bed, this time purposefully curled over on his side, his back arched, his legs out in front of him, slightly bent at the knee like a giant comma.

There could be no stiffening up as he rested.

———

The full effects of dehydration were beginning to set in and Valerie wondered how much longer she could last until her organs started shutting down. The hunger had fled not long after the kidnapping, too much adrenaline and panic suppressing the appetite until eating wasn't really a concern. Well, it *was* a concern, but she knew the body could go weeks without food, if needed. It'd cause damage, potentially, but she would survive.

She needed a drink of water.

Redsaw still hadn't moved.

———

Gabriel only stirred once while he slept, at least, so far as he could recall because it caused a brief wake up. He didn't remember if it hurt or not when it occurred. Now, he lay there dozing, doing his best not to think about how he felt.

He drifted off, echoes of the names Redsaw and Valerie somewhere drifting amongst the darkness.

"Get. Up," the voice said but Gabriel didn't know from where.

A strong piercing scent like sharp mint went up his nostrils and seemed to land a spike into his brain. He cracked open his eyes.

The figure in gray stood over him.

A moment of debate and Gabriel opted to not *shift* because he didn't want to give himself away.

His ragged Axiom-man uniform was tossed on top of him.

"Get dressed," the figure said.

Gabriel still didn't power up. Perhaps he could pretend he was an Axiom-man cosplayer or something and not the real deal.

"I said get dressed." The figured touched him at a place where his neck met his shoulder line. A sharp pain roared through his upper body.

As the pain faded, he clutched his suit. "I'm not—"

"He moved faster than anticipated. Get dressed. You need to go."

Gabriel glanced down at his gear. When he looked up, the figure was gone.

Chapter Twenty-three

The temperature on the roof slowly grew warmer. It wasn't long until Valerie's clothes clung to her skin, and the sweat wasn't from panic. She looked at the silver towers. Nothing about them had changed.

Redsaw remained on the ledge.

What she wouldn't give for a drink of water right now.

A low droning rumble came from the streets below. Subtle, firm, and there. Though she couldn't be completely sure, Valerie thought she heard screams rise on the air.

Redsaw now stood on the corner of the building. From behind, she could tell he held his hands in front of himself but what he was holding, she didn't know. Upon further searching her surroundings and the buildings nearby, she recognized she was on top of Owen Tower. Did Mr. Owen know about this? Was he in on it? Did Redsaw somehow blackmail the rich guy into allowing him to construct whatever these towers were meant to be?

Water. *Give me water.*

She knew it wouldn't come.

———

Redsaw held his hands out slightly in front of him, enough distance between them and his body to allow what was about to happen to happen. His fingers crackled with red energy, its raw power not only coming from within but from without as well. Whisps of red electrical cloud, small strings and threads on the air, began to rise from the streets and made a direct line toward him. The moment the first surge of red power hit, Redsaw's fingers locked.

Relax, he thought. *Let it come.*

Twirls and swirls of red energy danced off the city streets, some coming from so far away that one moment they weren't there, the next they were visible. The swirling incoming power increased in ferocity as it gathered and surged into Redsaw's hands. The power remained there, in his fists, at first. Even with the amount he was holding at the moment, he could easily blow a hole big enough through a building to make it come crashing down.

"More," he said and splayed his fingers. Red, crackling whisps of raw energy floated up from the city streets, the power filling his arms and seeping into his torso. It wouldn't be long until he filled himself completely.

All that death. All the riots. All the murders.

It was harvest time.

Redsaw let the power flow into him and grow and grow. He did his best to suppress the incoming onslaught of power, shove it down and make room for more.

Last time when he opened the Doorway, he had to commit each murder himself. But something happened during the last couple of kills back then, something he should have noticed with the other murders but didn't. Each removal of life created a small but tangible burst of red power, the red, he assumed, because the person had died at his hand. Back then, the power came into him and that was eventually what led to the initial opening of the Doorway of Darkness. After, when it was decided he had to open it again, Redsaw carefully observed each kill. Not only the demise of his own victims but even watching other killers having their blood-soaked way with someone else. It was probably his powers that allowed him to see it, but upon death, a white electric-like series of sparks ran up and down the body. He didn't know if it was the soul or some final electric outburst of the nerves, but it lingered.

He had left that body alone on purpose back in Toronto and kept an eye out for the authorities to show up to take it away. But that hovering aura of electric energy remained. As he heard the ambulance en route, Redsaw had stuck out his hand and discovered he could draw that energy in like a magnet.

It was there in Toronto that he figured out how to next open the Doorway of Darkness, and in such a way, that it could not be closed.

Not ever again.

———

All Valerie could do was sit there in a slump, weak, her body past the point of thirst with nothing but cotton in her mouth. She wriggled against her bonds but was unable to even wiggle a few millimeters never mind actually attempting to free herself.

She glanced over her shoulder after a thin beam of red light fired past her and traveled toward Redsaw, where he seemed to be gathering it in his hands. More and more whisps of smoky light sped past her, all of them coming up from the streets below and from off in the distance. Seeing powers at work was nothing new. She'd had plenty of exposure with Gabriel, but this was unique, at least to her, to see the reverse—power flowing *into* someone instead of out of them.

What's he doing? she wondered. She glanced at the silver columns and noticed each was not standing completely upright. They angled partly inward, each peak dipped toward the center.

High, and right above her.

———————

Each jolt of energy that flew into Redsaw's hands made him slightly recoil. It was one thing to grow in power over a single death, it was another to receive power from thousands. Truth was, he wasn't sure if even he could contain it.

"Gods are limitless," he said as he took in another shock of energy. "I will be filled."

Lights, streaks, whisps, balls of energy zipped into his hands, filled his arms, filled his torso, filled his legs. The surge of power sent a tremor through him and he focused on maintaining his footing while the rest of his body seized. The extreme volts of dynamite power crept up his neck and boiled through his veins, surging through every vessel, nerve, and cell. Convulsing with pure red power, he cocked his head toward the sky and screamed. His entire vision filled with bright red light and the heat of its sheer awesome strength poured forth from his mouth as his body tried to dispel the extra it contained.

Redsaw clamped his mouth shut, keeping as much power in as possible. Beams of hot red energy gushed from his eyes. He squeezed them shut, not letting a drop escape. But the sensation of power when the energy blasted from his eyes was new. *This must be how that wretched blue boy feels when he unleashes his power.*

He turned his head toward Valerie, eyes still closed. He didn't have to see her to know she was terrified.

———————

Valerie ducked and fell over onto her side when a shot of fragmented light whipped past her. Flows of targeted energy kept coming from below and entering Redsaw.

Another burst of moisture sprung up from her skin, coating her in a humid film of sweat.

This was not panic.

It was heat.

It took a moment for her dehydrated brain to catch on, but she realized she was laying down in the middle of an oven.

The columns were conductors, and Redsaw was *the* conductor of them all.

Redsaw opened his eyes, the energy now a red film across his vision. The convulsions eased but his entire body vibrated as if he had inserted his whole being into an electrical socket. Valerie stared at him wide-eyed, mouth agape. He looked down on himself and his entire body was covered with a thick layer of red light as dark as blood.

If you fail me, you will die. The master's voice was so clear, so precise, each word annunciated with extreme articulation. It was louder too, bolder, a voice with authority that had to be obeyed.

It was almost time.

The streams of red powers flowed in as Redsaw made his way to the middle of the roof.

Those black boots never made a sound when they came toward her. The moment Redsaw was next to Valerie, all sound on the rooftop ceased.

He reached down, grabbed hard around her neck, and pulled her weakened body off the roof and held it aloft before him. He raised his other hand, throbbing contracting and expanding pulses of bright red energy glowing from his fists. The burning heat of his touch made the skin of her neck boil, the burning quickly going from one to a hundred in a matter of seconds.

Screaming, her voice somehow getting through a parched throat, Redsaw shot forth a blast of power into one of the columns. In less than a second, it began to glow a harsh red, a perfect crimson, bright, lit, almost beautiful.

Redsaw pointed at another column and dumped energy into it as well. The two beacons hummed from the heat and whatever other power that surged through them.

Two, she thought. *And three more to go.*

Tears spilled out of the corners of her eyes as her neck burned.

Axiom-man hadn't needed to search for Redsaw. The man in the black cape made it obvious where he was. Owen Tower's roof was aglow in red light and a shimmering metal. He hoped Oscar Owen was aware of what was going on and called in help. Then again, maybe it was best that no one came. Whatever was happening, he had the feeling it was long from over.

Five metallic columns shot forth from the rooftop like a five on a die. Axiom-man made out two people near the middle column. One was in black, so Redsaw. The other . . . he knew. He didn't want to know, but he knew. It could only be one other person.

Valerie.

Axiom-man kicked on the speed and headed toward them as fast as he could, thankful his aura helped protect his bruised body and even secured it a little bit by the extreme adrenaline-like rush he always felt when powered up.

Redsaw held her up by the neck.

Axiom-man's heart raced at what he might do.

———

The streak of bright blue light coming straight his way from the sky was unmistakable.

Redsaw eyed the columns.

He eyed Valerie.

He eyed Axiom-man.

He brought his free hand in close and let a beam of energy flow out to form a sword.

———

"Almost . . . there," Axiom-man said. The light coming from Redsaw's hand, the glow of his fist around Valerie's neck.

Heart rate spiking, pounding fast and hard inside his ribcage, Axiom-man did all he could to get there as fast as possible. The moment he entered the rooftop's space, Redsaw brought the sword down in a violent slash.

Axiom-man's flight cut out, and he fell to the roof feet first and collapsed to his knees. He wanted to scream. Wanted to cry. Wanted to blast the hell out of Redsaw and tear every atom in his body a part.

But he couldn't move.

Just like Valerie, when her body fell to the rooftop. She didn't move and she didn't have to. The deep cauterized gouge that tore open her torso said it all.

There was a flash of black and a strong sense of disorientation when Axiom-man looked about the rooftop. Had he passed out? Had the shock . . . . No, he couldn't have been out for longer than a second, if that. He didn't know what just happened inside him but Valerie's body reminded him.

In the dead quiet space, the crackling noise of the red energy funneling from Valerie into Redsaw's hand went into silence. Redsaw pointed both hands toward the top of the middle column and the entire rooftop went off in a blast of silent fiery red light. Its brightness faded to the deep dark crimson of blood. All that stood out against the dark red was the burnished bronze-like color of the columns, each growing hotter and brighter with every passing moment. Their light went from bright red to orange to yellow to stark white. Pouring forth from their tops was sparkling red energy, each column connected by these beams of power. The thicker the red energy ribbons grew, the less the white the columns became.

Like rain, shots of red energy dripped from above, each bolt sending a scorch mark into the roof, some even piercing Valerie's body, desecrating what was supposed to be respected.

It could have been denial. It could have been the guilt. It could have been the sheer burn stabbing Axiom-man's heart, but he didn't know what to say or do. He wanted to lash out, wanted to put every bit of power he had into Redsaw and destroy the man. He wanted to do it slowly so the man suffered but he also wanted to do it fast and hard because the man deserved to die now!

Instead, there was no movement and not for lack of love or care.

It was love and care that kept him frozen . . .

. . . because it was love and care that drove him.

Love for Valerie.

Love for the city.

Love for his fellow human being.

And right now, the most important one of them all, was dead.

He took to the sky.

————

Gunn squealed his squad car over the curb and onto the sidewalk of Owen Tower. He jumped out and looked up.

The sky tore open.

CHAPTER TWENTY-FOUR

Time.
Patience
Observation.
Analysis.
Method.

Oscar Owen knew these principles all too well as a businessman. Putting them into practice had led to his success and so became a way of life both professionally and personally. Redsaw knew these principles too. He knew because Oscar told him. He knew, because he *was* Oscar Owen and Oscar Owen was Redsaw. If anything, Oscar had slowly faded over time, with thoughts and energy put toward enhancing his Redsaw abilities, learning about them, studying them, testing them. He maintained his physical health through Karate and strength training. And he maintained Redsaw's health through murder, torture, and destruction.

Beams of spikey, crackling red energy spewed forth from the silver columns, only connecting at the top and not shooting out new branches, as if each column was attempting to reach the other in an effort to enhance it.

Redsaw floated up and to the side of his creation, observing the red, dense piercing lasers that crackled and burned between the columns. What he was about to do next only worked in theory. He had done minor practice with a very small-scale model just to see if the idea would work. The honest truth was, he wasn't sure. The experiment was on such a small scale the results were mixed and strictly observations limited by the human eye. Despite his resources, Oscar could not find any sort of device that might be able to gauge or even read his powers. Machines couldn't read what they didn't know.

This has to go right, he thought. *I cannot fail my master. I know I will die if I do. I can only hope he somehow guided me throughout this.* He wasn't sure how. So far as he was aware, his master was confined to the realm of the Doorway, but there was also evidence along the way that indicated his master could reach into his world now and then.

If you fail me, you will die. The master.

"I won't fail you," Redsaw said quietly. He floated up to the bubbling electric red light and slowly extended his hands. *Careful.* He extended his fingers. Immediately, shots of red energy burst from his hands and zapped along his fingers, the beams of energy across his digits never ceasing but dancing along between his fingers. Redsaw moved his hands and contracted then expanded his fist over and over, the red energy following the motion of his hands.

It's working. Time. Patience. Practice. The power in his hands could be controlled and not just used as death rays. He had dexterity with it, control over it.

It was his.

Redsaw held his fingers aloft and let direct beams of red energy flow from the columns and begin to fill him. Almost immediately his sight was blinded behind a shield of red light. He widened his eyes as another wave of power swept through him. His entire body was aglow with violent crimson energy, its force and ability swelling within him, his head swooning, the electric signals in his brain beginning to be interrupted, thoughts slowing, confusion setting in.

Hands.

Focus on the hands.

Redsaw flew up and drew his fingers together, each hand like a spear, then focused the red power from inside his body up from his feet, through his legs, his torso, his arms, palms—fingers. A blood-red blade spewed forth from his fingers, coalescing into a sharp flat knife he would—Before he could even attempt control, the tips of the blades from his fingers pierced through the air. The beam only traveled slightly outward before seeming to disappear into the night air.

He knew. It *was* working.

Redsaw took to the tip of the combining power coming off the columns and let the energy enter him through his legs, his body becoming a conduit, the outpour thin blades from his hands.

He cut like that night long ago in the MTS Centre. He relaxed as best he could and let his mind be taken over by instinct as the red energy coursed through him. The red blades tore into the fabric of space and time, cutting open reality and finally, oh so finally began opening the Doorway again.

Redsaw cut.

The Doorway slowly started to form.

———

Barely conscious, Valerie weakly screeched as strips of power ripped and zapped above her head, bouncing between columns without pattern.

Chaos.

Pain.

The smell of burnt meat.

She pulled her dry tongue from the roof of her mouth and whispered, "Help." She didn't know who she was talking to, didn't know who would hear her, didn't know who—It could have been her squinted eyes, but she thought she saw a blue star coming toward them.

———

Axiom-man pulled his flight to a halt the second he got near the glowing columns of red energy. Immediately, a rush of what felt like fluid swept from inside one side of his head to the other, forcing him to lose all sense of where he was or even why he was here. His body went limp like jelly and all he saw was red light and . . . and . . . he needed an anchoring point, he needed . . .

"Oh no." The words were barely a breath.

Valerie. There. Lying in the middle of the columns.

"What? Why?" Again, words of breath.

His stomach lurched and he had to float away from the red. He couldn't maintain focus, could barely breathe, could barely—Valerie!

Axiom-man looked upward and a sharp pain pierced his heart when he saw an opening begin to form and the shadow of a man creating it.

A scream. Feminine. Helpless.

Valerie.

No, not Valerie. Not anyone. There was nothing but silence and Axiom-man didn't know if Redsaw was causing the quiet or he was too affected by the red and his senses were starting to shut down.

If he entered the field . . . he didn't know what would happen. He had never seen so much of Redsaw's power before, not even that night long ago when Redsaw opened the Doorway of Darkness. Axiom-man had barely survived that. There was no way he was going to survive this.

Time . . . it didn't seem to be the river it was a moment ago. Axiom-man's internal clock felt stuck in a moment, a scene, a frame.

Valerie.

She was going to die if she stayed there.

He was going to die if he went to her . . . but if he survived, if he could somehow get her out, get her to safety, then . . . then . . . why was he here, again? Who?

"Wake up." The words barely came out. "Focus. Think. Wake . . ." He drifted further away from the red and could only imagine the storming hurt in Valerie's heart and the tears in her eyes if she saw him moving back. Whatever strength she had left was being used to hang on.

"Oh no," he breathed again. He knew what this was. He knew what this *is*.

Worst of all, he knew what he had to do . . .

CHAPTER TWENTY-FIVE

. . . CHOOSE.

And he didn't know the right choice.

In this place of silence, Valerie danced across his mind. His first meeting her, her ignoring him, the fun times trying to impress her despite purposefully acting like a dork. The times she showed signs of warming up to him, the times she caught herself doing so and held back. The time . . . he held her as Gabriel Garrison, and the time he held her as Axiom-man. The time she found out who he really was. A talk. A kiss. A friendship as foundation for so much more. Cuddles. Late nights. Movies. Popcorn. Tender holds and hand squeezes. Her brown eyes. Her gorgeous wavy brown hair.

Her skin.

Her touch.

Her love.

Valerie.

Valerie Vaughan.

———

She couldn't move any more. The strength to budge was gone and Valerie was afraid any overt motion on her part would trigger one of those red energy beams and send one her way.

That blue star.

Her blue star.

Why were you so far away?

Please, don't be afraid. Gabriel . . .

———

Redsaw poured the power out, flying high, flying across, ripping as much into the fabric of space as he could and as large as he could. Dense streams of red power flowed from the beacons, drawing all death and power from a city gone crazy. He could only imagine the rotting bodies on the streets, the glorious actions of person turning on person, producing blood.

Death rose off the streets of Winnipeg, manifesting in more red power mixed with black cloud.

Redsaw never let the little blue star out of his sight nor did he leave unattended the girl below.

It would only be a matter of time, and the longer Axiom-man waited, the more assured the Cobalt Crusader's defeat.

———

Whisps and crackles of red energy mixed with black cloud swept past Axiom-man, each one brushing past him causing him to drop another foot down toward the ground far below.

This had been his plan all along. The city, the riots, the death—all of it meant for right now. He felt like a fool. How could he not see this coming? How could he not expect Redsaw to be secretly working on regaining whatever power that seemed to have been lost.

The opening above the beacons of glowing red silver cracked and burned against the night sky, black clouds spewing forth from its maw, drifting out and over the city like a death-blow storm cloud.

Valerie. The roof.

Cops at the base of the building; no one moving.

THE SUMMONING

Axiom-man closed his eyes and went inside himself.

————

It was only moments after Gunn had pulled up that the captain started squawking on the radio. He didn't care. Let the man ramble and get mad. All Gunn knew looking up at the violent red and black storm above Owen Tower was there was nothing he nor his men could do.

He glanced to the right to the small blue glow in the distance. He took off his hat and said, "Finish this."

————

Through the red haze, Gabriel's blue form was a faded purple, drifting and drifting away as the heat from the columns seared Valerie's skin and made her scream with the little strength she had left.

————

Redsaw ceased his work. The power from the Doorway of Darkness would take care of the rest, its realm open, its power flowing forth.

He eyed the girl and flew down toward her.

When he landed beside her, the faded blue star in the distance drew closer.

————

Though he could barely maintain coherence, Axiom-man kept his target in sight. Though his powers were as forceful as he could muster, he concentrated and *shifted* inside, as if activating them anew. He'd never attempted *shifting* after he'd already shifted but found it was like digging deep into a run, pumping your legs as hard as you could despite your muscles burning and begging for relief.

The blue aura around him glowed brighter, its layer thickening to double. He didn't know if his aura was borrowing power from another of his abilities, or if it was him generating it himself but it helped.

Brain starting to come around, his vision sharpening, his heart ached when he saw Redsaw next to Valerie. Fire, fear, and aggression consumed him. He dare not touch her. He dare not come near.

Redsaw was right beside to her now.

He bent down.

———

Skin beginning to bubble, Valerie was on the edge of blacking out from the pain. A heat so pronounced made itself known throughout her muscles, her bones, her veins. Her wounds.

Black hand around her neck.

Upward movement that only caused her to weakly scream, a coarse scream from the pain. Then a voice.

"Valerie." It was Gabriel. It was Axiom-man. It was . . .

. . . Redsaw.

———

Axiom-man dove into the realm of red energy, forcing back the pain, the nausea, the pounding ache that ran through his bones.

Redsaw looked at him without expression, then back at Valerie.

A red blade formed from his fingers and cut her throat.

———

Redsaw dropped the body then noticed a figure in a dark gray outfit with hood and cape, dim shadows over a mask, stare at him. The figure turned and dropped off the edge of the building.

———

Axiom-man plowed into Redsaw as a burst of red energy thundered from the columns, all branches and streams pointing upward and fueling the Doorway.

Redsaw threw Axiom-man to the side. Axiom-man's strength vanished and he fell to the roof, collapsed in a heap. All he saw was the blasted cement of the rooftop and endless glowing red.

He summoned as much power as he could to his eyes, blue energy coated his vision then faded purple, then turned red as if he hadn't pulled from his powers at all.

Valerie's body lay there, blood pooled all around it as if he tore her open after slashing her . . . . He tried to crawl toward her, to reach out, to touch her, to feel her one more time. Instead, black hands picked him up and one of those hands ran its fingers through his hair.

"You're nothing special, are you?" Redsaw said.

Axiom-man glanced up, noticing strands of what appeared to be his own brown hair leaving his fingertips.

My powers. They were there. He felt them inside. Somehow this Ground Zero point had *shifted* him away from his abilities. Axiom-man focused and *shifted*, a surge of strength quickly filling him then leaving him. Not here. Not in this place. Redsaw . . .

The hands reaffirmed their grip on his shoulders and swung him around so his body faced skyward.

"Do it again," Redsaw said. "Or is the mask interfering?" He reached toward Axiom-man's face.

No! Axiom-man kicked on the power again and this time, drew and drew from it to maintain it. A bright blue aura surrounded his body and strength and viciousness filled his limbs.

Redsaw was going to die.

Axiom-man drew deep and concentrated as much power as he could into his eyes. "I'm . . . going to . . . kill you."

"Yes." Redsaw grinned.

The silence never left. And Redsaw didn't make a move.

It's time, Axiom-man thought, tears dampening his mask, the heat from the environment quickly drying the fabric.

Redsaw gave his mask a tug and the second he did, Axiom-man opened fire.

Redsaw vanished. The immense dome of crackling red power with the massive Doorway of Darkness beyond opened up, revealing the Doorway in full.

The realm of red and black cloud, an eternity of death and damnation.

And he was firing directly into it. A violent push from behind sent him rocketing skyward, and as much as he tried to fly against the force, he couldn't break its momentum.

His aura tore from his body and spiraled into the Doorway. The energy left his eyes, and all strength left his limbs until he was nothing more than a doll heading hard and fast skyward. He tried to look down, to see Valerie one last time, but he couldn't turn his head from the speed.

The Doorway drew closer, and it'd only be a matter of seconds before he went in . . .

. . . powerless.

CHAPTER TWENTY-SIX

THE MOMENT THE blue light left Axiom-man's body, Redsaw manipulated the red energy surrounding his enemy and wrapped ropes of power around the man in the blue cape. With a violent tug, he yanked the energy ropes down, pulling Axiom-man down with them. He slammed the Cobalt Crusader's body into the rooftop then glanced up. Whisps of faded blue and purple disappeared into the Doorway.

The glowing red columns began to tremble at first then escalated into an all-out shake. Bits and chunks of hot silver began to burst forth from their mainstay and they began to buckle. Redsaw gathered all his strength and launched as much power as he could into the columns, the red intensifying in power and heat.

A column to his left snapped about three quarters of the way up and fell in. So did another somewhere behind him.

Redsaw eyed Axiom-man's body then eyed Valerie's roasting form. He picked Axiom-man up by the collar and dumped him on top of her, Axiom-man's face to hers. Redsaw tore off Axiom-man's mask.

"Face her. I don't care who you are." He slowly shook his head then started into the sky, heading straight for the Doorway.

He flew faster past the columns as they collapsed inward and a fiery red explosion blew the roof off the entire building.

All that mattered was the Doorway.

He was finally home.

"Look out!" Gunn shouted at his men as roof debris fell from hundreds of feet up. He jumped back into his squad car for protection and tried to drive away. The engine wouldn't start. The entire dashboard was dark.

Gunn looked out the window and down the street as dark clouds fell like rain onto the city. "Oh my word . . ."

He got out of the car and, on wobbly legs, tried to get as far away from the area as possible. Bright orange lit the area around him when the top of Owen Tower went up in flames, then the floor below it, then the one below that, fire blowing out windows as it descended toward the street.

Gunn took a deep breath and screamed as loud as he could, "Run!" He tried to lumber his large form as far away from the exploding building as he could. He didn't know how long he or any of his men had before the thing might fall in on itself.

The flames roared.

The black clouds fell, pooling in the streets and wafting into every crevice.

Gunn rounded a corner and pressed his back to the wall. He squeezed his eyes shut. Winnipeg was finished. He had been right since the start. Metahumans were dangerous no matter what side they were on.

He peered out into the street, tears running down his cheeks as the city died.

"It's over."

About the Author

A.P. Fuchs is the author of many novels and short stories. His most recent books are *Axiom-man/Crimson Cloak: Scarlet Synergy*, *Zomtropolis: A Record of Life in a Dead City,* and *Giganti-gator Death Machine: Triple Feature.*

Also a cartoonist, he is known for his superhero series, *The Axiom-man Saga*, both in novel and comic book format. Please visit **www.canisterx.com** for more on this series. For his webcomic, *Fredrikus*, about a down-and-out anthropomorphic dog in a dystopian sci-fi world, please go to **www.fredrikus.com**

As well, be sure to subscribe to A.P. Fuchs's YouTube Channel at **www.youtube.com/@apfuchs** for books, comics, podcasts, stories, and more.